THE
SECRET
SHADOW

THE SECRET SHADOW

Copyright © 2023 by Bethany Atazadeh

All rights reserved. Printed in the United States of America. No part of this book may be used or reproduced in any manner whatsoever without written permission except in the case of brief quotations embodied in critical articles or reviews. This book is a work of fiction. Names, characters, businesses, organizations, places, events, and incidents either are the product of the author's imagination or are used fictitiously. Any resemblance to actual persons, living or dead, events, or locales is entirely coincidental.

For information contact :
https://www.bethanyatazadeh.com

Cover design by Stone Ridge Books

First Edition: June 2023
10 9 8 7 6 5 4 3 2 1

BETHANY ATAZADEH

GRACE HOUSE PRESS

Copyright © 2021 by Bethany Atazadeh

d e d i c a t i o n

To those still learning how powerful you truly are…

Also by Bethany Atazadeh

THE STOLEN KINGDOM SERIES :
THE STOLEN KINGDOM
THE JINNI KEY
THE CURSED HUNTER
THE ENCHANTED CROWN
THE COLLECTOR'S EDITION / BOX SET

THE QUEEN'S RISE SERIES :
THE SECRET GIFT
THE SECRET SHADOW
THE SECRET CURSE

THE NUMBER SERIES :
EVALENE'S NUMBER
PEARL'S NUMBER

MARKETING FOR AUTHORS SERIES :
HOW YOUR BOOK SELLS ITSELF
GROW YOUR AUTHOR PLATFORM
BOOK SALES THAT MULTIPLY
SECRETS TO SELLING BOOKS ON SOCIAL MEDIA
PLAN A PROFITABLE BOOK LAUNCH

SIGN UP FOR MY AUTHOR NEWSLETTER

Read the first half of The Stolen Kingdom for free, receive exclusive bonus content, a free short story, helpful tools for fellow writers, other behind the scenes updates, and more!

WWW.BETHANYATAZADEH.COM/CONTACT

1

"THIS WILL BE YOUR room." Prince Shem unlocked a solid wood door and handed me the gold metal key. With a glance I could only describe as thinly-veiled annoyance at the two guards on his heels, he added to me, "I'll show you where you can put your things." He stepped inside, waving for me to follow.

Before I could step forward, both guards moved between us. "Your highness—" one of them began, with a sharp glance in my direction.

Without a word, Shem took my hand and gave it

a tug, forcing his guards to allow me past.

He put an arm around my bare shoulder, making my skin tingle. His ornamental armor pressed against my side, cold and solid. "I'm not expecting an attack in Jezebel's empty room," he remarked dryly. "But I promise I'll call for you if the furniture rises up against me."

Both guard's eyes locked on me, narrowing. Their prince might not see me as a threat, but they certainly did. I couldn't tell what bothered them more—that I was a common Jinn from the acropolis or that I was allowed to be alone with the prince without being vetted.

Shem winked at me, ignoring them. When the door swung closed, he added softly, "It seems you're a bit of a legend already."

I scoffed.

"It's true," he insisted. "They may have noticed that I took you on many of my latest adventures to the human world…" He gave me that co-conspirator grin I'd grown fond of. Those warm blue eyes carried a disarming friendliness that was impossible to ignore. Paired with his sharp jawline and disheveled black hair—and of course, being the prince of Jinn—he was naturally irresistible. But his genuine interest in his people—in *me*—was what truly drew me in.

Blushing, I said, "A few little adventures hardly makes me a legend."

"On the contrary." He laughed, rubbing the back of his neck. "I apologize in advance, but the Guard seems to have marked you as someone to watch."

My brows rose. I tried not to react further, but my heart rate picked up. "Wonderful," I muttered.

"Take it as a compliment." Shem winked and added, "Legend."

Some of my tension faded at the nickname. I laughed and changed the subject, "I believe I was promised a tour?"

"Ah yes—" His grin disappeared briefly as he put on a mock serious expression. Bowing, he waved an arm, "—Welcome to your room."

Turning to take in the space, I tried not to gape at it like a common Jinni from the acropolis. If my younger self had visited the castle, I'd have sworn this space was the king's own room. My entire acropolis apartment could've fit inside.

"Bed, wardrobe, desk, attached bathing room, window… all the standard features," Shem teased, but they didn't feel standard to me at all.

Above us, a chandelier almost as tall as me hung from the high ceiling. Both the desk and the wardrobe he'd mentioned had delicate designs carved into the dark wood hinting at how expensive they must be. And the bed was a huge four-poster with a canopy over it and a white fur rug beneath.

As I moved toward the window, my jaw dropped at the view of the lavender garden stretching out in the distance.

I felt like an imposter.

Shem and I had met less than two months ago, by accident. Or rather, by unintentional design. After betrayal forced me to turn on my only friends, Shem was tasked with finding them, and we'd been drawn together during the search. But while he spent hours working with his Guard to find the lost Jinni children, they'd been under my bed in lizard form the whole time. Until the last second, when I'd slipped them into the human world right before the portal was closed—and left them behind.

I didn't deserve to be here.

Shem shifted behind me, making the wood floor creak, but he didn't speak and I didn't turn around. The grief came at the most inopportune times.

Another minute passed before he cleared his throat. "If you don't like it, please don't be afraid to speak up. We have many other rooms—"

"Oh no." I turned to reassure him. "It's not that

at all. I'm just… overwhelmed by your kindness."

"It's nothing." He grinned and added, "Legend."

At the ridiculous nickname, the tension in my shoulders eased. I laughed softly. "Thank you."

I didn't know what else to say, but the corners of his eyes wrinkled as he smiled back, and I knew he understood.

A few days ago, Shem had sent a formal invitation to join his council and come live at the castle. When he'd first heard my father was gone and I had nowhere to go, he'd offered it immediately, but I hadn't truly believed him until that day. Lots of people made promises, but Shem actually kept them.

I'd packed my bag that same night.

Partly because living in the castle was a dream come true, but mostly because I didn't have anywhere else to go. Not after what I'd done to my friends—and my father.

As I'd left my apartment for the last time, I'd tucked that empty jar—the one I'd used to trap them—beneath the clothes in my bag. I wanted it with me. Not as a memory, since I'd never forget what I'd done, but more to remind myself never to let something like that happen again.

Setting that same bag down on the bed, I stepped

subtly away from it. Though I returned my gaze to the garden, I barely noticed the Jinn strolling along the walking paths.

I never wanted to hurt anyone with my Gift again.

If I wanted to avoid repeating my past, no one else could ever learn my secret.

Not even Shem.

My eyes locked on his reflection in the window as he leaned against the wardrobe, running a hand through his hair and rubbing the back of his neck. "If it's not the room, is there something else bothering you?"

I swallowed hard, forcing a smile. "Nothing that can be fixed, I'm afraid." Taking a deep breath, I tried to say something close to the truth. "I just wish I didn't need your generosity as badly as I do."

"It's not your fault your father abandoned you," he was quick to say with a rare frown.

But it was.

Clearing my throat, I ignored his comment, gesturing around us instead. "The room is incredible. Thank you." The trembling in my voice wasn't from the view.

He smiled and accepted the subject change. "I haven't shown you the best part yet."

Shaking off my dark thoughts, I gave him a curious glance.

"Are you aware of the protection spell over personal rooms in the castle that prevents traveling?"

Most Jinn could travel long distances in the span of a breath. It was considered one of the lesser Gifts—unless a poor Jinni didn't have it.

Unfortunately, it also meant that there was no such thing as a locked door to a Jinni who could travel right through it. That's why most Jinn used the protection spell for privacy. It acted as a lock, preventing unwanted travel into personal spaces.

I nodded. "The acropolis uses the same spell."

"Well, the royal family created a second spell that forms a loophole of sorts."

Intrigued, I raised a brow. "Oh? I've never heard of it."

"You wouldn't have." He came to join me at the window. "It's reserved for those the royal family trusts. And well-guarded for obvious reasons. There wouldn't be much point to the spell preventing travel if *everyone* in the castle knew how to get around it."

He glanced my way with a smile and caught me studying him. I blushed as his words sank in: *Reserved for those the royal family trusts.*

I ducked my head. *Does he trust me?* I wanted to ask, but I wasn't nearly as forward as he thought I was. I chewed on my lip instead.

"Come. Let me show you." Shem waved a hand at the wardrobe. Patting the dark maple wood, he leaned casually against it. "This particular spell creates a 'room' within a room. You simply need something large and enclosed, like your wardrobe here."

I stopped close enough to feel the heat from his arm next to mine. He smelled like a pine forest with the barest hint of cinnamon. It tickled my nose. I leaned a bit closer, pretending to inspect the detailed carvings, and my long black hair brushed his arm. He didn't seem to notice. This close I could see a hint of dark stubble.

I startled when he spoke, "Unlike your room, this smaller space doesn't have a spell preventing travel."

"The loophole," I whispered, coming back to the conversation. My lips parted. *Impressive.*

Shem's eyes flicked to my lips and then back to the wardrobe.

For weeks now, there'd been this tension between us. Brief touches, stolen looks. Half the time I wondered if I imagined it, but the other half—

moments like this—I wondered if there was something between us.

Was the wardrobe a declaration? A way to reveal how much he cared without saying it out loud?

I took it in with new eyes.

It stood on four little legs that lifted it off the floor, making it slightly taller than Shem. Through the intricate carvings, the inside was visible.

It was empty now. But once I unpacked, it'd barely be half-full. I only owned a handful of dresses and a few pairs of sandals. Nothing like the grandiose outfits I'd already seen in the castle so far. Everyone else on Shem's council likely had ten times as much.

"You'll receive a stipend for more clothes," Shem said, as if he could read my mind.

My cheeks filled with heat. I wrapped my arms around myself, wishing I could burn this simple day dress.

"I'm sure you don't need it," he rushed to add. "It's just that council members are often required to attend extravagant events, so the royal family feels it's only right to compensate everyone for that."

The royal family. Did he distance himself on purpose? The uncertainty of it all, constantly going back and forth on what things meant, made my mind spin.

"Thank you." I acknowledged the offer, trying to hide my shame. I gestured to the wardrobe—the more personal gift. "It's incredible."

He shrugged off the praise. "It's useful. The enchantment against travel is intended to keep unwanted guests out. This way, you're able to keep the privacy benefits, but you don't lose your freedom to travel *unobserved*." He emphasized the last word. I didn't need him to elaborate to know he was referring to the castle gossip.

"I love it." Daring to place a hand on his arm, I smiled up at him. "How does it work?"

"Step inside," he directed, opening the thin door for me. I did, turning in the small space to face him. "Now, close the door behind you to seal the room." He pressed it closed as he spoke, and the wardrobe door clicked softly shut.

Through the gaps in the decorative wood, I stared into his pale blue eyes.

A heartbeat passed.

Instead of traveling to test out my new freedom, I gently pushed the door back open and stared at him, gathering the courage to ask, "Why would you do something like this for me?"

I wasn't sure what I hoped he'd say.

But I couldn't help wishing he'd stop the usual Jinni hinting and be straightforward for once.

I wanted to believe there was more to our relationship than simply a prince and his new council member.

Shem waved a hand and smiled. "It's really not that special. Everyone on the council has a loophole spell."

My little bubble of hope popped.

Deflating, I hid my disappointment behind a forced calm.

"Consider it a thank you," he continued, moving to the side so I could step out of the wardrobe. "It's one of the many privileges of being one of my advisors." His cheeks dimpled as he grinned, and I forced myself to smile back.

This wasn't a romantic gesture after all.

While I hadn't met all of them yet, Shem had almost three dozen council members.

It stung.

Turning away, I touched the carvings on the wardrobe door and gently closed it, avoiding Shem's gaze. I wanted to kick myself for getting my hopes up.

"Let's continue your tour, shall we?" He smiled,

seemingly unaware of my inner turmoil.

I pressed my lips together in an imitation smile.

The two members of the Jinni Guard trailed after us as we walked. "The rest of my council, as well as my mother's and father's councils, all reside in the south wing as well," he began, gesturing down the long hallway.

Doors led to individual apartments, just like the acropolis. Except here in the castle, the hall had lush blue carpet, solid limestone walls in a crisp shade of white, and expensive décor carefully placed in small alcoves. There were dozens of vases, paintings, and even a full suit of ornamental armor that likely belonged to a former king.

We passed an open seating area with comfortable lounge chairs and heavy drapes beside floor-to-ceiling windows. Shem continued past with a familiar nod to those seated inside, but he didn't stop.

As we reached the heart of the castle, he gestured to the hallways on either side of us. "The royal family lives on the east side. And most of the long-term servants live on the west."

I tilted my head back to stare at the stained glass window four stories above us in awe. Sunlight filtered through, lighting the large, round room with dozens of bright, flickering colors.

"The north wing holds the largest rooms, including the dining hall, which I'll show you later." Shem's voice came from further away, and I hurried to catch up before he noticed me dawdling. "There's a smaller throne room, meeting rooms for all of the councils, and over here—" I spun to look where he was pointing, at a heavy-looking set of double doors twice as tall as him, "—is the grand throne room."

As we continued on, Shem glanced over. "It can be a bit overpowering at first."

I cleared my throat. "It is. But I'll get used to it." I'd make sure of that—I'd spend my nights exploring in lizard form until I knew these halls better than anyone.

A few Jinn headed toward us from the opposite direction. All eyes fixated on my bare, sandalled legs. Here in the castle, the dress code was clearly more formal.

The first woman wore a sleek, backless gown, made of a dusky blue that grew darker as it neared the hem, looking exactly like the sky at twilight. Lights twinkled along the bottom half of the dress like stars. Beside her, the other woman's vibrant red dress had feathered sleeves that reminded me of a cardinal. Between them strode a man in ornamental armor. Unlike the sharp silver armor of the Jinni Guard, worn from head to toe, this shining surface was a soft, gold metal that would never hold up in a real battle. It was also studded with diamonds. Definitely not intended for combat, then. It was flashier than anything I'd ever seen Shem wear.

Even before I'd come to the castle, I'd heard of the fashions here, but seeing it in person was an entirely different experience.

They bowed to the prince, ignoring me entirely.

I raised my chin, gazing past them and pretending not to notice.

"The council meets in the east wing," Shem said, picking up the tour where he'd left off. "The royal family's quarters are also in the east wing, so the Guard will require you to pass through a checkpoint each time you enter."

"Is that where we're headed now?" I sounded shy. Childish. Gritting my teeth, I pulled my shoulders back, determined to fake confidence if I couldn't find it on my own.

"It is." Shem placed a hand on my arm, guiding me toward the stairs.

He let his hand fall, but it'd drawn my attention to my simple attire once again. I had on a single gold armband and my short white day dress with otherwise completely bare arms and legs. Did the stipend Shem had mentioned include jewelry as well? My own small collection was cheap in comparison. I'd be lucky if I could afford any of the latest fashions here.

As we entered the east wing, the thick carpet changed to a deep red to signify the royal family. We walked in silence, until finally Shem cleared his throat. "I should probably share before we arrive, that there's been a bit of contention in my council over my decision to bring you on."

I stiffened.

"Nothing to be concerned about, of course."

Swallowing, I nodded, but I didn't believe him for a second. "What're their concerns?"

He hesitated. Gesturing for his guards to wait, we walked a bit further, before stopping out of hearing. "I'll be as honest with you as you've been with me," he murmured. "There's talk that you won't know the customs and that you won't respect the way the council works. Some think it's disrespectful to the institution and the monarchy. And a small number feel that your upbringing…" He faltered again.

"My upbringing?" I repeated, frowning. "You mean, growing up in the acropolis?" Our little apartment was just one of thousands within the thick acropolis wall that surrounded the city. Though it was on the outskirts, that didn't make us less civilized than anywhere else in Resh. "Surely not everyone on the council grow up in the castle?"

I expected him to say no, but he slowly nodded.

"Oh…" I shrunk back. I'd worried before about fitting in, but now I felt certain I wouldn't.

"Most of my personal council is around our age," he continued. I tried to follow his train of thought, unsure how that was relevant. "What I'm trying to say is, they aren't set in their ways. They may have formed an opinion now, but once they meet you, they'll see you're more than capable."

Am I though?

I didn't know how to respond to that, because I was half-convinced they were right. Instead, I changed the subject again. "Is the entire castle spelled so you have to walk everywhere? Or do you travel sometimes?"

Shem chuckled, waving for the guards to rejoin us as we began walking again. "Fair question. We often stroll for a bit of exercise, but traveling is perfectly acceptable in the main halls. It's only the personal and private rooms that are spelled to prevent traveling in and out. Oh, and the throne rooms and the dining hall."

Chewing on my lower lip, I hummed my understanding.

"Here we are," Shem said before I could ask anything else. "You'll likely remember some council members from when you were here before." He gestured toward a set of double doors in a hall with a guard posted outside.

"Gabriel," Shem called as we drew closer. "You remember Jezebel?"

"Of course," he said, bowing stiffly.

We'd met before? His face wasn't memorable. *It doesn't matter. He's just a guard. They're not important.*

Gabriel's dark eyes narrowed almost imperceptibly. He looked down his nose at me, raising a single brow, then turned to Shem, dismissing me. "Most of the council is in attendance, your highness," he said as he pulled the door open for us.

"Very good." Shem gave him a nod as we passed.

The door nearly clipped my heels as it closed

behind us, and I jumped, whirling around. Gabriel's back was turned, but I could've sworn he'd done that on purpose.

The door clicked softly shut.

Shem stopped in the small entryway unexpectedly. I almost bumped into him.

"Did they teach you how to guard your mind during your discipline years?" he asked without explanation, standing closer than Jinn usually did.

His nearness distracted me for a second. I nodded, faintly remembering the teaching. I'd been good at it, but we'd only spent a few days on the training before moving on. "A bit. Why?"

He cleared his throat, leaning close enough to whisper, "Guard member's Gifts aren't usually disclosed unless necessary, but you should know Gabriel has a minor ability to read minds."

I sucked in a breath, tensing.

What was I thinking in the hall? I tried to remember, my thoughts scattering frantically. Had I thought of my shape-shifting Gift? My breathing sped up. I put all my energy into slowing it back down. I didn't think so? I couldn't remember!

Hair rose on my arms as another thought occurred to me, and true panic kicked in. "Can he read minds through the door?" I glanced back at the dark, stained wood.

"No," Shem reassured me, and I blew out the breath I'd been holding. "Most, if not all mind-readers need a visual for their Gift to work. And like I said, Gabriel's Gift isn't terribly strong."

"But he's on the Guard," I whispered back. Which meant it was strong enough. It was *mind-reading* after all. The Gift I'd feared most when trying to decide if I should come here.

"He usually doesn't hear anything, unless a thought is being broadcast."

Like mine probably had been.

They came to me then.

Just a guard. Not important.

I sighed. Had I already made an enemy before the morning ended? I'd find out soon enough.

"Ready?" Shem waited for me to nod, before leading me out into the council room.

I'd been here once before. I'd had a temporary seat on the council as we planned a mourning event to honor my missing friends. The room was familiar, with its long wall of books, dark blue velvet furniture, long mahogany tables, windows that stretched from floor to ceiling, and an upper level with a balcony and more bookshelves.

THE SECRET SHADOW

This time, however, at least two dozen Jinni faces stared back—they'd been waiting for us.

2

GABRIEL'S WORDS CAME BACK to me: most of the council *in attendance*. Shem had planned an event? As I trailed him to the center of the room, I wished he'd given me a bit more information. What was expected of me?

"Come, sit with us," a nearby woman said when I hesitated. She had sleek waist-length hair that matched her black dress and gold accents that complemented her yellow-gold eyes. I vaguely remembered meeting her before.

Warily, I took the seat. The sharp points of her

dress poked me in the shoulders as she shifted to make room. She didn't seem to notice. Smiling, she whispered in a slightly condescending tone, "I wouldn't expect you to remember us, but my name is Jerusha. This is Milcah."

Turning to glance at the woman on my opposite side, equally young and pretty, she gave me a closed-lip smile before returning her attention to Shem.

I tried not to stare at her decadent dress. It was also black, with a delicate trail of white flowers along one side from head to toe and a plunging neckline. Was everyone wearing black? I glanced around the room, confirming they all were. Was there a dress code I wasn't aware of? I frowned as I turned back to Shem. His armor gleamed silver and his crisp shirt and pants were white. Not a trace of black on him. I rubbed my forehead, trying to make sense of it. It was almost as if they were dressed for mourning.

Shem finished speaking with a nearby Jinni and stepped to the front of the room, clearing his throat. "Thank you, everyone, for taking time to be here today. Most of you remember Jezebel, I hope?"

The Jinn around the room smiled at me pleasantly enough. Maybe Shem was worried for nothing.

He nodded to Jerusha and Milcah on each side

of me. "Thank you both for taking the initiative to welcome Jezebel to the council. I will place her with your circle first, and potentially long-term if it's a good fit."

I raised a brow at the unfamiliar term, hoping it was a good thing.

"I'll keep my speech brief, as I'm sure you're all excited to get to know our newest council member. Feel free to mingle. The noon meal will be delivered shortly."

His easygoing leadership clearly trickled down to his council, as they immediately began talking and the volume in the room rose. Before I could think of something to say to the women next to me, Shem joined us.

"I probably should've asked you ladies first," he began, pulling up a tall blue-velvet chair to sit with us. "I do apologize. I got caught up in the moment."

They glanced at each other so briefly I almost missed it. Jerusha waved him off. "Nonsense."

Milcah nodded in agreement. Both of them leaned forward, smiling, drawn to the prince like dragons to their prey, and Milcah said to him, "We're honored, in fact, that our circle would be your first choice."

THE SECRET SHADOW

They probably didn't realize I had no idea what they were talking about. I cleared my throat. "Circle?"

Milcah was making eye contact with someone across the room, gesturing for them to join us. Jerusha didn't seem to hear me either, smiling at Shem instead. "No doubt she'll be a good fit, once she... adjusts to our customs."

"The circles are smaller work groups within the council," Shem explained when they didn't, focusing on me. "I pair Jinn together on smaller projects so the council can work on multiple issues simultaneously. Occasionally we come together for bigger concerns, but often you'll work more closely with a specific few on the council: your circle."

I tried not to flush from embarrassment at how obvious that was once he said it. "How many others are in our particular circle?"

"Just a few," Jerusha said vaguely. To Shem she added, "We'll introduce her, don't worry about a thing."

Hesitating for a second, he smiled and thanked her. "I'll be nearby if you need me," he murmured to me before standing to face another Jinni waiting at his shoulder.

"Tell us about the acropolis," Jerusha jumped

back into conversation before he'd finished turning, grinning at me. "What's it like living by the river? Did you have discipline years? Or did you skip those and stay at home to work?"

I blinked at her words, which were mildly insulting. It didn't *seem* intentional…

"Yes, do tell," Milcah added, ignoring the nearby Jinn who'd approached us.

The flood of questions overwhelmed me almost as much as the dozens of eyes. Should I introduce myself to the others? Or answer Jerusha? It seemed like Shem valued resourcefulness, so maybe Jerusha and Milcah expected me to take the initiative with meeting everyone.

"Ladies," a Jinni tsked as I wavered in indecision. She slipped through the crowd, lowering herself elegantly into the chair where Shem had sat. "Don't be ridiculous. You're acting as if you've never been outside the castle to see the acropolis with your own eyes. And all Jinn attend their discipline years. Even the lowest Jinni deserves to learn with their peers."

Once again I didn't know if I should be insulted or thankful for the rescue.

When she smiled at me, it *seemed* genuine.

"Not at all, Dorcas," Jerusha replied, and her brows drew together as she turned to me. "I do apologize if my questions were intrusive. I simply wanted to get to know you better and hear about common life outside the castle."

Her apology appeared authentic as well, despite the snub. It was as if they couldn't help themselves. Or maybe they were good at hiding their true feelings…

"The acropolis apartments are certainly modest, compared to the castle," I admitted, lifting my chin. I met their gazes through sheer force of will. Whether it was well-intentioned or not, their scrutiny was uncomfortable. "We still have many of the same luxuries, as well as a beautiful view of the River Mem. Incomparable, really." I wasn't as skilled in subtle jabs, and the poke at the castle views landed awkwardly, leaving a beat of silence in its wake.

"I'm sure you miss it." Dorcas patted my arm, managing to sound superior even when offering comfort.

Jerusha reached forward to touch my bare knee. "You won't miss that wardrobe though," she teased. "I'm sure you're dying to get out of those old things and wear something more fashionable."

Heat flashed through my whole body.

I wrapped my arms around my waist as I mumbled, "Yes, of course."

"Give the girl a rest," Milcah inserted herself with a mothering look in my direction. "She's intimidated enough by her drastic change in circumstances without you pressing her for information. Aron, what is your circle working on?"

At first, I was grateful for the reprieve. But as they discussed terms I'd never heard before, my body tensed, forming the beginnings of a headache. I was in the center of the group without a clue what we were discussing. If they asked me to weigh in on a subject, I'd look like a fool. Fortunately, no one did. It was as if they'd forgotten I was there altogether.

The noon meal arrived, and the group dissipated, leaving me alone with Jerusha and Milcah again when Shem rejoined us.

"I trust everyone is making you feel welcome?" he asked, glancing at the ladies. I swore something like a warning flashed in his gaze as he addressed them. Something almost protective. My stomach fluttered.

Their eyes landed on me.

"Absolutely," I replied with a small smile. I still couldn't tell if their offensive comments were calculated or accidental. What Shem had said before we'd entered came to mind, about the council not being thrilled about my joining them, but I still hoped that wasn't the case for everyone.

Shem's shoulders relaxed. As we all moved to the dining table to eat, I tried not to frown. He was doing everything he could to make a place for me, but in the end, it was up to me. It was normal to have a little awkwardness when meeting new people, but I'd make friends soon enough. Maybe even someone I could trust. At least, I hoped so.

AFTER A WEEK, however, I was quickly losing hope.

Every interaction with council members led to embarrassment. I laid awake at night pulling apart each conversation, but I couldn't put my finger on the reason for it. No one acted unpleasant toward me on purpose. It was more that I seemed to naturally make a fool of myself. Sometimes, I didn't need their help at all. They'd laugh and someone would tell me, "Not to worry. You'll adjust to the castle eventually."

Today, after an hour of conversation, I needed a moment of peace. I'd hidden behind some bookshelves on the balcony.

Below, a low woman's voice drifted up to me. "The poor girl. It's not her fault she's so simple. Growing up in the acropolis doesn't afford someone the luxury of good taste. Or *intelligence*."

Her listeners laughed.

"I truly don't understand why the prince spends so much time with her."

"No," a second voice agreed. "And I can't say I like it either."

"Neither do I. Perhaps there's something more there than meets the eye, but I cannot fathom what it might be…"

As I listened, I flushed hot and then cold.

Footsteps sounded on the stairs.

They were heading toward me.

I needed to leave before I burst into tears.

If I could've traveled away, I would have, but the council rooms had the usual spells that prevented it.

Which meant my only way out was to walk right past them.

Keeping my expression cool and composed—or as close to it as I could under the circumstances—I swept out from the bookcases and brushed past them without a word, chin high.

THE SECRET SHADOW

It was Jerusha and Milcah.

"Oh my," Jerusha stage-whispered. "Do you think she heard?"

Ignoring the muffled laughs that followed, I strode down the stairs toward the door, past the blurry shapes of the Jinn on the first floor.

"Jezebel?" Shem's voice floated toward me as I twisted the door handle. I ignored him too.

I couldn't let him see me like this.

My feet hit the thick carpet of the hallway, and I traveled.

Reappearing outside my room, I shoved through the door, slamming it behind me, and burst into tears.

I didn't belong here.

I knew it. They knew it. The only one who didn't was Prince Shem. But if he hadn't figured it out yet, he would soon.

A soft knock sounded on the door seconds later.

I barely heard it at first, through my sobs.

Another knock.

This time, I caught myself, silencing my cries so they couldn't be heard through the door, though the tears didn't stop flowing.

"Jezebel?" It was Shem's voice. "I don't mean to intrude, but you looked upset."

I hesitated.

Swiping at the tears with my sleeve, I tried to force a calm I didn't feel before I swung open the door.

"May I come in?" he asked, mostly as a formality, since I'd already stepped back to let him enter.

The door clicked softly shut behind him and we stood in silence. I tried to think of something to say, staring at his polished silver boots that matched his decorative armor.

"What happened?" his voice was a little unsure, something I hadn't heard from him before.

I raised my gaze to his. The concern in his eyes made me give in. With a sigh, I chose my words carefully. "I think you were right about the council not wanting me here."

He stood, agitated. "Who's making you feel unwanted?" Beginning to pace, he ran a hand through his unruly hair and turned back to me. "Give me their names. I'll make certain they don't mistreat you again."

Instead, I pressed my lips together. If I told him about Jerusha and Milcah, he'd remove me from their circle, but would any other circle be better? Especially if they thought I was complaining about them to Shem? Unlikely. At least in this circle I knew who I couldn't trust. "It's not important," I murmured, lowering my gaze.

"Jezebel." Shem's tone was fierce. He knelt beside the bed until I met his gaze. "If someone is causing you pain, you *must* tell me."

I pressed my lips together, attempting a small smile. "I promise I'm stronger than you think. I'm probably a little homesick, that's all."

Shem gave me a look that said he didn't believe me for a second. Rubbing a hand across his face, he blew out a breath and leaned against the window ledge. He stared out at the gardens below.

After a moment, I joined him, touching his fingers lightly. "They just need more time to get used to me. I'll sway them, don't worry."

The tension in his shoulders eased slightly. He sighed, curling his fingers around mine and squeezing once before letting go. "I know you will."

We stared out the window without speaking. Below, at least a dozen Jinn strolled along different garden paths or lounged on wooden benches. I could only make out a few recognizable faces from this distance.

I lifted my gaze past them to where the enormous River Mem flowed through the middle of the city. It passed through the acropolis, which circled the city, entering on one side and exiting on the other.

Even from this distance, the fierce waters raged and churned, reflecting my inner turmoil. I kept my face smooth, not wanting Shem to see. While I pretended confidence with him, I'd learned not to trust others once before, and I shouldn't have hoped it'd be different here. I wouldn't expect to make any friends on Shem's council. If anything, I'd already made some enemies.

"It's my fault you were unprepared." Shem broke the silence finally, shaking his head. "I should've warned you."

"Of what?"

"Life in court involves a lot of… maneuvering. It's something I've always lived with. I'm afraid I've grown so used to it, that it didn't occur to me I should give you some training."

"All right," I said slowly, frowning. "Train me."

Whatever that meant.

He smiled a little. "There's that charmingly stubborn streak of yours." He gestured for us to sit.

I sagged onto the bed as he pulled up the desk chair to sit across from me. "It's all about learning how to twist their words before they can twist yours. After time you'll begin to phrase things more carefully as well, which will remove their own opportunities for insult. You are just as intelligent as they are—more so. Your lack of pretense shouldn't be mocked. It's a noble quality more Jinn should have—it's what drew me to you in the first place."

I tried not to scoff. That felt like a lie to make me feel better.

"Truly." He must've seen through me. He leaned closer, more sincere than I'd ever seen him. "You've just never required the skill of manipulation before."

After a pause, he added more softly, "That's something I very much admire about you."

* * *

TWO MONTHS LATER, Shem's declaring how he felt had turned out to be a rare occurrence. But I *had* begun to find my feet in the council's slanted conversations.

Sometimes.

As I strolled through the gardens, enjoying the sweet smells and the shade along one path, I refused to admit I was avoiding my circle today. I simply needed some fresh air.

Whether that was true or not, it didn't matter.

From the opposite direction, a small group of council members approached, glancing at each other.

"Jezebel," Milcah greeted me from the front of the group. "You must be taking a glory walk as well."

Someone snickered at my confused expression. "She doesn't know what that means, dear."

Milcah sighed, patting my arm as if I was a child of eight and she was an elderly old woman, though we were both an equal eighteen-years-old. "It's a castle term, I do apologize, everyone else would know it." They weren't being very subtle today. "It essentially means taking full advantage of a beautiful sunny day because you can afford to—that would explain why you'd never heard of it before."

Soft chuckles came from the others as I flushed.

Before I could answer, a member of the Jinni Guard flashed onto the path before us. "I come from the castle with a message from the prince for his council." Though I was closest to him, he handed the note to Milcah instead. He didn't give me a second glance before traveling away.

Without a word, Milcah read the message, then passed it to the Jinni behind her. She traveled.

"What does it say?" I asked, as the next man read it and imitated Milcah, handing it over and disappearing as well.

Irritated, I refused to repeat myself. I waited for my turn, but when the last council member finished the note, he simply let go and vanished, leaving me alone.

The paper fluttered to the ground, then took off down the path, carried by a sudden gust of wind.

I was forced to chase it.

Grunting, I snatched it up, pulling the hair out of my eyes as I tried to catch my breath and read the note:

There's been a discovery. Council meeting at your earliest convenience.

—Shem.

Short and straightforward, they could've easily conveyed what it said before they'd left.

The real message from all of them was clear: I was *not* one of them.

Though their scorn was usually more veiled than this, their intent was obvious. And the Jinni Guard went out of their way to confirm the sentiment, as if despite the simple upbringing many of them had, they were somehow also above me.

I did *not* belong.

The worst part was, I felt the same way.

3

"I NEED TO SEE the prince." I strode down the hallway, stopping before the double doors that led to the council chambers. As expected, no one had waited to make sure I was coming.

Thick red carpet muffled my voice and the clink of polished silver armor as Gabriel, one of the Jinni Guards, shifted his crystal spear to block the entrance.

Neither his armor or weapons were nearly as intimidating as his expression, however. Impassive, yet unapproachable, it hid the Gifts that lay beneath

THE SECRET SHADOW

the surface, but I hadn't forgotten what Shem said: *a mind-reader.*

Most castle residents spent years learning to shield their minds, while I'd only truly begun practicing two months ago. I was still in many ways an untried beginner.

I envisioned a wall around my thoughts as a mental defense, like I'd been taught back in my discipline years. It took effort to carefully lay brick after brick until the imagined wall grew thick and strong. Was it enough? I worried he could somehow hear my heartbeat quickening.

He lowered his gaze to mine. Silence stretched between us, making my eye twitch.

It took everything I had not to look away.

If there was another way to see Shem today, I wouldn't be here.

But he was on the other side of that door.

Despite the fact that Gabriel knew me well, he still kept his crystal spear barred across the gilded gold door, unmoving. "Business?"

"Council meeting." The same thing I always said. I could share details, but like most Jinn, I preferred my privacy.

The prince's council was smaller than both the king's and the queen's. Somewhere between two and three dozen Jinn. But he used his for more meaningful ventures than planning frivolous parties like his mother or getting caught up in politics like his father. Since I'd joined his council a little over two months ago, we'd searched for missing Jinn, closed wayward portals, discussed the growing attacks from the Khaanevaade, and dealt with spells, enchantments, and other equally important things.

Since Gabriel wasn't part of Shem's council, however, none of these things were any of his business.

"Take a seat, and I'll be with you shortly," he replied finally.

It's going to be one of those days, is it?

"I'm in a bit of a hurry," I said with false cheer, speaking slowly as if talking to a child. "Maybe you could practice your castle defenses on someone else today?" I didn't need anyone to tell me that he was yet again attempting to read my mind, stalling in case I slipped and gave him an opening.

"Apologies," he said, though he barely hid the glint of enjoyment in his eyes. "Occasional delays are just a precaution for the prince's sake."

And if it's for the prince, how can I argue? I pressed my hands against my skirts so he wouldn't

THE SECRET SHADOW

notice when they trembled.

I'm strong enough to keep him out. Or at least, that's what I told myself, trying not to think what might happen if I dropped my guard and let him see something from my past.

No doubt that's exactly what he hoped for, and the reason he made me wait so long and so often.

Despite living in the castle for months now, visiting the prince's council rooms almost daily, Gabriel and the others in the Jinni Guard still didn't like or trust me.

Maybe they never would.

Though there were comfortable chairs conveniently placed along the wall for instances like this, I didn't sit like Gabriel requested—that would only fuel his misguided power-trip.

But I did take a step back, crossing my arms and drawing in deep breaths for patience. This wasn't the first time Gabriel or the other guards tried to put me in my place, and it probably wouldn't be the last.

That didn't make it any easier to ignore his eyes on me, though.

Ever since I'd arrived, I'd been on their bad side. None of my offenses were intentional. But in some ways, Shem's council was right, I was an outsider. I didn't understand the customs of the castle. I was bound to break some rules.

"Do you take issue with all of Prince Shem's council members? Or just me?" I muttered under my breath, trying to hide the growing sense that maybe he *should* keep me out.

He acted as if he hadn't heard.

In fact, he wasn't even acknowledging my presence anymore, staring blankly at the opposite wall.

The arrogance of the Guard, I was used to. But the poorly veiled contempt always reminded me I might never find a place here. How many years would pass before they'd consider me one of them?

Briefly, I imagined striding down the red carpet that led back to the heart of the castle, then on to my room. It was tempting. Shem would probably never learn that I'd been here in the first place. But I didn't want to hide any more than I already had been.

I also didn't want to complain to Shem. He'd done so much for me already. The problem wasn't just Gabriel anyway; all the Guard members had taken on his opinion of me. If it wasn't him denying me entrance, it'd be another.

I was gripping the sleeves of my dark green, floor-length gown unconsciously. With effort, I relaxed my fingers. I turned away from Gabriel, pretending to study the artwork hanging on the wall across from us instead.

Smoothing out the crumpled fabric, I let my arms hang loosely so I wouldn't be tempted to wring the poor dress any further. I'd shifted the fabric to give it a slight shimmer of gold beneath the first layer, with thicker threads of gold woven through the bodice and sheer sleeves.

It was nothing like the simple short dresses and sandals I was used to. Yet it still didn't measure up to the stylish dresses some of the other council members wore—gowns made of seemingly liquid gold, fabric that rippled like fire, a skirt full of flowers that bloomed on their own, feathers of all shapes and sizes, mermaid scales... really anything that glowed, swirled, or seemed impossible. Spells always enhanced them somehow.

I could only do simple shifts to my clothing before my abilities lost their effect, but truthfully that was for the best. Anything more extravagant and someone might question how I could afford it with the modest clothing budget Shem had provided.

This dress was purchased from that budget, which meant that technically it was from him. I pressed my fingers into the sheer fabric along my sleeves trying to draw strength from that.

He wanted me here, even if no one else did.

That was the reason I didn't give up or complain, despite over two months of this treatment.

"Gabriel," a female voice said behind me in a warm tone that suggested a smile. I recognized her voice instantly. *Jerusha.* As one of Shem's council members since the day he'd begun working with a council, she and the prince had grown up together in the castle. She'd let me know on my first day here that she and the prince had been friends for years. *Chased after him for years, more like it.*

I turned to face her, momentarily stunned, as usual, by her dress. The top piece was an ebony corset. Decorative gold chains delicately held it up, wrapping around her neck and shoulders. But my gaze was drawn to the skirt, where the black flowed like lava into molten red, orange, and even small flickers of yellow fire as it billowed out and *moved* around her legs.

Her eyes slowly trailed down my own dim, green dress, hanging flat and lifeless. A slit along one side revealed my favorite pair of sandals, wrapping around my feet and calves, but they were plain leather. No embellishments or decorations.

THE SECRET SHADOW

A flush of shame rose to my cheeks. Under her gaze, my clothes seemed childish. She'd never wear something so simple. But no one on the council shared their clothing spells with me, and I had too much pride to ask. It'd only fuel their gossip about how little I knew about castle life.

Gabriel lifted his spear, allowing her to pass.

My whole body clenched.

Jerusha's mouth twisted up at the corner. She didn't bother to vouch for me or reprimand Gabriel, though he was clearly making me wait longer than necessary. Turning the door knob, she chuckled softly as she entered. "Perhaps we'll see you inside."

The door closed with a heavy thud.

I shrugged as if I couldn't be bothered to care, struggling to keep my hands loose and relaxed. Forcing my chin up, I leveled a bored look at Gabriel.

I could've sworn his lips twisted up slightly in a smirk.

He and Jerusha both seemed to take pleasure in undermining me—everyone in the castle did. Always imperceptibly. Like this, in a way that couldn't be called out without sounding foolish.

If I put in a complaint about Gabriel, he'd only protest that he was doing his job. He'd swear he gave me the same treatment as anyone else: a routine check for threats. Worse, he might take my unwillingness to be detained as an opportunity to question my loyalty to the crown.

On the other hand, if I accused Jerusha of allowing the slight, she'd place a hand over her heart, as she said to Shem in a condescending tone, "I do apologize, your majesty. I didn't realize the girl needed a babysitter."

They knew what they were doing.

I stood awkwardly in the quiet hall, ashamed, waiting for Gabriel to stop denying me entrance to the council.

This could last a few more minutes, or, if he was feeling spiteful, a few more hours.

I'd had enough.

I refused to spend any more time standing humiliated in the hall.

My voice broke the silence, startling both of us with the forcefulness. "This seems to be either a deliberate slight or a disturbing loss of memory." I almost broke off there, but forced myself to continue, pretending confidence I didn't feel. "Since I can't *imagine* a member of the Guard being intentionally disrespectful to a royal council member, I have to assume it's the latter." I gave an exaggerated sigh, shaking my head at Gabriel. "Perhaps the prince should be informed. I was under the impression the Guard needed to be sharp-witted." I started to turn away. "I suppose I'll have to let him know that not everyone in the Guard is up to the royal family's standards."

I strode down the hall.

"Wait," Gabriel called after a few steps.

I turned, arms crossed.

Grudgingly, after a long pause, he pulled back his spear. He didn't apologize, refusing to even meet my eyes as he allowed me to pass.

I gave him as much space as possible, holding back a shiver as I slipped through the large door.

Smoothing my face as I entered the large council room, I made sure not to show any sign of my embarrassment from the hallway.

A couple Jinn glanced up from where they were browsing the dark mahogany bookshelves or seated in the surrounding blue velvet furniture. A large fire roared in the hearth that stood as tall as some of the Jinn nearby.

Dust motes danced in the light shining in through the wall of windows. It gave the whole room a magical feel.

On the balcony above, a murmur of conversation

drifted down, but otherwise the room was fairly empty. There were a handful of council members with Prince Shem, gathered around one of the large tables.

Milcah was the only one who saw me coming. She wore a gown that made her look like midnight incarnate—a deep blue with diamonds flickering all across it like stars in the night sky. The diamonds trailed along the low neckline heavily to draw attention there, as well as lined a cape that looked like a shooting star flowing behind her.

She stood as I entered, drawing nearer to the prince where he hunched over something at the long table. Whatever she murmured was too soft for me to hear, but it distracted him from my approaching footsteps. Her silky black hair cascaded down her shoulder and arm to land on the table, creating a thick curtain that blocked my view of whatever they were working on.

Frustration mixed with shame, but I kept those feelings hidden as I crossed the council chambers to join them.

Clearly I was late for some new finding.

Despite being paired with this circle for months now, none of them cared if I attended this meeting or

THE SECRET SHADOW

not.

Face burning, I didn't say a word about the exclusion. Whenever I did, Milcah would cheerily say something like, "Oh this? We didn't call an official meeting darling, we just *happened* to all be here. No need to get all worked up over a chance conversation." Or in this case, since Shem *had* called a meeting, she'd probably ask why I'd dawdled. I pictured her turning my delay into a question of my commitment to the council.

I'd rather not be forced to swallow another story like that today, so I kept my mouth shut and joined them.

Dorcas glanced up next. She stood beside the table instead of sitting, likely because she didn't want to crush the vivid red flowers that circled her white skirts. They grew along layers designed to look like hills, leading up to the massive red mushroom cap that circled her tiny waist and emphasized her hips. Sparks of light dusted the skirts and bodice, giving everything an otherworldly glow. Her dull blue eyes darted between me and the prince, as if she was torn between acknowledging me and pretending not to have noticed my arrival, but she didn't have a chance to decide.

"Jezebel," Jerusha's cheerful voice rang out in

the library as if she hadn't just seen me in the hall. She was louder than necessary, making Laban startle and drop his pen.

He turned toward me with a wide grin, taking off his reading glasses. I could never decide if his attentive gaze and abundance of questions were due to interest or ulterior motives. Since he spent time with the Jerusha and Milcah, I tended to assume the latter.

His decorative armor gleamed silver with gold embellishments, just as much the height of fashion as the women. The stomach muscles on the armor were chiseled to look extremely defined, which made me want to roll my eyes. Laban rarely even walked anywhere if he could travel, much less took the time to build his physique.

When I finally allowed myself to sneak a glance at Shem, his eyes were already on me.

"Someone found a *Kathenoth* and delivered it to the castle," Jerusha said before Shem could greet me. "It's a thrilling find—oh, I don't suppose you know what a Kathenoth is, do you, dear?" Unlike Milcah's tactic of edging me out of conversations and opportunities, Jerusha had a different strategy. Whenever possible, she found a way to make me seem simple. Useless.

I sent her a scathing look behind Shem's back, but I didn't expect any less.

"Everyone in Jinn knows about Kathenoths," I replied with a sweet smile, as if I hadn't even noticed her attempt.

A Kathenoth was simply a fanciful term for a journal that you *meant* for someone to read.

As Jerusha passed the small book to me, I hid my distaste and took it. It felt heavier than it really was, like the secrets it held weighed it down.

Every paranoid Jinni with enemies—which described almost everyone in the castle—kept at least one Kathenoth. Usually they were strategically placed somewhere they could easily be found if their owner vanished.

Pretending to study the book, I swallowed.

It wasn't a perfect fail-safe. There was still a chance no one would happen upon it, or at least, not in time to reverse the damage done.

I offered it to Laban, who was closest to me, wanting to be rid of it.

"I've already had a turn," he said. The others refused it as well. Shem reached out to take the little book, and I held back a sigh of relief.

He set it on the table and slowly flipping through

the pages. We looked on, waiting quietly. I kept my eyes on his hands, ignoring the others, until a servant stepped up. Passing the book to Jerusha, he stood to speak with them.

A Kathenoth offered protection from the *Shakach* spell—often referred to simply as the forbidden forgetting spell. Shakach was a hard word to translate, but it meant something between ignorance and withering. And that was exactly what it did: it erased a Jinni from existence, even in their own mind. It made them—and everyone else—forget who they were, filling in the holes left behind until they weren't even noticeable anymore.

Jerusha stroked the pages of the little journal where it lay open on the table, drawing my attention to the delicate handwriting, before she snapped it shut.

I shivered.

Without a Kathenoth, you might never be found.

It occurred to me that the others were uncharacteristically quiet as well, and I risked a glance around the table. Perhaps they were equally unsettled.

If a Jinni wrote down evidence of their existence—as well as what to do with their

THE SECRET SHADOW

belongings if the discovery happened after memories grew too fragmented and distant to repair—those they left behind had a very small chance of breaking the spell.

That was the key to a Kathenoth: having someone who would find it.

As the servant spoke with Shem, I snuck a glance at his profile.

I wasn't sure I did.

Though I'd never tell Jerusha or the others, I hadn't bothered to make a Kathenoth of my own because I was afraid. If I left bread crumbs behind, there might not be anyone to follow them. The only person who'd care if I disappeared was Shem. And only three short months of memories needed to be erased before he'd forget me easily.

What if no one had found this little book? The embellishments on the cover were beautiful, but nothing guaranteed it would be noticed. What if it'd gone undetected for years, until it was too late, and the memories were impossible to bring back?

Shem turned back to us.

Jerusha's lips were turned up in a cat-like smile.

Now that I'd had time to think of an insult, I wished I could've recommended she make ten Kathenoths since she seemed so concerned about being forgettable.

I might've come up with the response sooner, if the discovery hadn't left me flustered.

Even when I'd abandoned my friends in lizard form in the jungle, I hadn't dared to do a Shakach spell on them.

Not only did it break our strict code of ethics, including the Three Unbreakable Laws, but it also came with consequences. The dangers of a spell like that weren't worth it. It could backfire and obliterate the memories of the spell-doer just as easily as the intended victim. Yet there were Jinn who disregarded the potential repercussions.

Stepping closer, I peered down at the little book.

It terrified me to imagine being erased from memory so completely that I'd never be missed.

Or rather, I'd never even be *remembered*.

I determined then and there to start a journal tonight. I'd leave it in the middle of my bed where it'd be impossible to miss.

"Interesting," I lied. "My Kathenoth is a similar color."

"Oh, darling," Jerusha tsked, interrupting my thoughts. She held a dramatic hand over her black leather corset and the gold chains that held it in place as she shook her head. "Don't tell me you only have *one* Kathenoth?"

4

I FLUSHED, FRUSTRATED THAT she'd somehow managed to turn that back around on me.

Jerusha would be merciless if she discovered I didn't have even one Kathenoth hidden for someone to find.

Keeping my gaze on the little journal to avoid looking at Shem and giving myself away, I wondered yet again if he'd feel the hole of my absence deeply enough to come looking for me, despite the lack of memories. Ever since arriving at the castle, my feelings for him had grown, but I still didn't know how he felt. I wavered between believing his feelings were there, beneath the surface, and at the same time, convincing myself that I'd imagined everything.

"Perhaps fresh eyes will help." Shem saved me from having to answer the taunt. "We've hardly made any progress on discovering the owner of this Kathenoth. Why don't you see what you can make of it?" He smiled and waved me forward.

His decorative armor was understated compared to the design of Laban's chiseled abdominal muscles, though it still included shoulder wings and a brace along each forearm. The metal gleamed in the light and had the royal family's insignia embossed across the breastplate.

His kindness encouraged me, even though after months at the castle, I now knew he offered this same consideration to everyone he met, not just me. It was a quality I both liked and disliked about him. Right now, his smile included the others equally, and I felt a twinge of jealousy.

Still, I stepped close enough that the sheer sleeve of my gown brushed his forearm. Catching Milcah's frown from the corner of my eye, I smiled up at him.

Laban's slight smirk told me he was equally aware of the tensions around this table.

The only one who seemed oblivious was Shem,

leaning around me to point at the open page where the handwriting was nearly illegible. "Listen to what it says here..." His warm fingers brushed over mine, distracting me slightly as he turned the page and began to read, "'I didn't intend to go to the anointing. But in the end, I made an appearance...' Do you realize what this means?"

He grinned at me, brows raised.

The anointing.

An anointing only took place before a Crowning Ceremony, which only happened twice in a century.

Every 50 years, on the last day of summer, the reigning sovereign of Jinn would remove the enchanted crown that enhanced their natural Gifts, strengthening them and affording them absolute control. The removal severed the enchantment.

If the ruler stood uncontested, they'd be crowned anew, but if an heir to the throne stepped forward, the ruler would concede the throne—and the crown—to their heir.

Though the last two centuries had passed with King Jubal wearing the crown, he'd made it known that he was preparing to pass it on to Shem this coming year.

Shem's Crowning Ceremony was still almost a

year away, but the anointing—one of the first steps that would lead to Shem's succession—had just taken place last month.

The night before the anointing, I'd been sneaking through the halls in lizard form, still familiarizing myself with the castle, when I'd caught Shem deep in conversation with his parents. Queen Samaria had been lecturing him, "It's time you grow more serious about preparing to rule. You're setting the example for all of Jinn."

King Jubal had chimed in, in a much harsher tone, "These little explorations were fine when you were younger, but it's time to give them up."

And Shem had.

Not only had he stopped inviting me to go on adventures with him outside the castle, but he'd also called an official council meeting the next day, speaking more solemnly than I'd ever seen him, "My father trusts that I will be the leader Jinn needs. As such, I plan to dedicate more time to the tasks he gives me. We will take on more duties as a council as well."

My brow had furrowed, but no one else in the room seemed surprised.

As the anointing came and went, I'd seen Shem less and less.

My depressing thoughts distracted me from Shem's question long enough for Milcah to beat me to the answer. "Your anointing was last month," she stated the obvious, making me want to roll my eyes. "And there hasn't been another in over a century. Which means that unless this journal is over a hundred years old—" she stroked the open page, which still looked brand new, giving the prince a sultry smile— "This Kathenoth was abandoned recently."

As she leaned back to lounge against the blue velvet chair, she ran graceful fingers through her dark hair and smiled at me innocently.

Laban scowled. "That makes this entire situation much more urgent," he said, leaning over the table. "If it's that fresh, there's still a very real threat until the one who cast the spell is found. What if one of us is next? Or the royal family?"

Someone willing to use the Shakach spell once wouldn't be afraid to use it again.

That sobered the rest of us, even the prince.

"It's impossible to know for sure whether or not the royal family is in danger," Shem said after a beat of silence. "Ultimately, there are many precautions in place to defend ourselves from such attacks, but I

THE SECRET SHADOW

will entrust this Kathenoth to your circle and have full faith you'll find the owner shortly."

There were layers of pressure within that statement. I wanted to find the owner for Shem's sake, but also for my own, to prove to the council that I was worthy.

I sank into an open chair. The others frowned and I realized it'd belonged to Shem. "So sorry," I murmured, moving to stand, but he waved me back into it.

"No apology necessary, I need a moment anyway," Shem said, brushing off my embarrassment. He strode across the room toward the windows where he began to pace.

Turning back to the table, four sets of eyes gazed at me with varying levels of irritation. It was hard to say if it was at the situation or at my claiming the prince's attention. Maybe they simply didn't think I was capable of solving the Kathenoth. But to avoid direct conflict, which was rarely done in the castle, I turned my gaze to the open journal on the table and began to read.

One page at a time, I poured over each detail, trying to get a sense of the owner. The one who'd been erased.

The library grew dark as the sun set. Candles

were lit to make up for the difference. I barely noticed the hush fall over the room as most of the council left for dinner.

"What do you make of it?" Shem leaned over my shoulder unexpectedly. His eyes, so light blue they were almost white like his mothers, met mine. In rare moments like this, when it was just the two of us again, it felt the way it had when we'd first met. I could almost feel a tangible thread connecting us, telling me I must mean something to him, because he'd come to mean so much to me.

"What do *you* make of it?" I asked to hide my surprise—I hadn't heard him return. I'd gotten so caught up in the writing that I'd even managed to tune out the soft murmur of conversation from the others.

In response, Shem sat in Milcah's open chair, which she'd abandoned at some point in the last hour or so to speak with Laban by the fire. Her eyes bore into me, but I ignored her.

"It's obviously a woman," he began. "And it seems to insinuate that there are multiple threats to her life." He flipped back a couple pages, still near the end of the book, where the writing stopped and the remaining pages were blank. He pointed to a blank space where a name should've been but the spell had erased it. "This would suggest she had good reason to be concerned."

I cleared my throat, and he paused, nodding for me to go ahead. "I noticed that," I began softly, hoping no one else would join us, in case I was wrong. "It's just… It's almost…" I searched for the right word. "Forced? As if the author is trying to mislead anyone who reads it?"

Shem's brows rose, disappearing under his unruly dark hair. Frowning down at the page again, he tilted his head and scooted closer, spinning the little journal to face him. "What makes you say that?"

Though Dorcas had long since left for dinner, Jerusha came to stand over us with crossed arms, trailed soon after by Milcah and Laban. I could almost feel them sifting through what they'd overheard to find a weakness.

I shut them out and tried to focus.

Milcah leaned in, wedging herself into the small space between Shem and I, under the pretense of studying the journal closer.

Reluctantly, I leaned back.

It was either that or press my face into her generous chest.

Another council member named Risha, with a

fiery orange dress the same color as her eyes, drew closer to our little group. Though she wasn't part of this particular assignment, Shem's excitement had clearly caught her attention. Whatever I said next was guaranteed to spread throughout the rest of the council and be twisted as it fit their needs—especially if I accidentally misspoke.

"It's in the little details." I cleared my throat again, lifting my chin and straightening my spine. "The beginning doesn't line up with the end... At first, the owner of the Kathenoth is smitten by a young man. She doesn't name him, but you can tell from the context that they spend a lot of time together. She also cites quite a few comments from family members against him... I think—" My mouth was dry enough that I had to swallow before I could keep speaking. If I was wrong, the others would love to rip me to shreds and declare me unfit for the council. They'd been looking for excuses to do so since I'd arrived.

Though I trailed off, Shem's frown deepened, as he reviewed the text in this new light. When I still didn't continue, he glanced up impatiently. "Please speak your truth, Jezebel. We have all made guesses in our time that required the inspection of others. No one will judge you for attempting to decipher what happened here. Your guess is as good as anyone else's."

Inhaling deeply, I hid my relief. They certainly couldn't judge me now, after *that* speech. At least, not openly.

"Here, she says she wants to leave Resh with this unnamed man for one of the smaller islands. He's mentioned on nearly every page. Then, suddenly…" I flipped a couple pages, finding the one that had caught my attention. "Here. The tone shifts. It sounds as if an entirely different person wrote the following pages, which doesn't make any sense." Jinn with Kathenoths didn't share.

"It makes me wonder…" I cleared my throat. "I think she made a decision to portray a different story on purpose."

"Why would she do that?" Shem asked and murmurs of agreement came from the others.

Ignoring their skeptical looks, I made my tone firm. "I believe the owner of this Kathenoth cast the Shakach spell over herself. "

Slowly Shem exhaled, dragging a hand down his face, shaking his head.

My heart sank.

I'd gone too far. Clearly I'd imagined it. Though

he'd barred the others from judging me, he was obviously forming a poor opinion of me himself.

"How did we not see it?" he whispered.

My breath hitched. "What?"

"It's impossible to miss, once you point it out," Shem said in awe, letting his gaze drift up to meet mine. An incredulous smile slowly stretched across his face. "It's such a risky move that it hadn't even occurred to me. Especially since it'd require additional protection spells to allow her to keep her own memories, while everyone else forgot."

I bit my lip.

When he said it like that, it sounded even more implausible. I began to question myself along with the others.

But Shem continued to nod and murmur to himself, as he flipped through the pages. "Yes. I believe that may be exactly what she did."

"You're not truly considering this story she wove out of nothing?" Jerusha protested.

Now that my heart rate was returning to normal, I let my lips curve into a smile.

Shem's response was polite on the surface, but his tone held an edge. "Where you see nothing, Jerusha, there is in actuality an extensive trail of breadcrumbs that Jezebel has found." He smiled at her to soften his words, but they cut off her objections just the same. While the prince was often free with his compliments—a fact that normally bothered me—I basked in Jerusha's annoyance now.

He wasn't done. "Jezebel, you seem to have an unparalleled ability to dig up the truth in texts where others see nothing."

My smile didn't slip, but a small part of me grew still.

My understanding came from my own secrets.

Suddenly, I wished I'd let someone else solve the Kathenoth, rather than put myself under the spotlight.

The eyes on me were like hot coals raking across my face.

Prince Shem stood unexpectedly with a relaxed stretch, smiling at everyone. "I believe that's our cue to retire for the evening. We'll still study the Kathenoth privately until we can break the spell and verify this story with a name, and I'll have the Guard review it as well, but I think we can all agree that there's no threat here. I believe the owner simply doesn't want to be found."

As we all turned to leave, Shem brushed my arm lightly, signaling for me to stay behind. Though

Jerusha, Milcah, and the other council members who'd joined us all likely noticed, they respected the prince enough to continue exiting.

As the door clicked shut, Shem turned to the fire, putting a little distance between us. Things like this confused me. Was he shy? Or maybe he wished to avoid any feelings he might have? Perhaps there were no feelings to evade in the first place. The clues he gave me could lead equally to both possibilities.

"I don't know how you do it," he said over his shoulder with a smile.

I shrugged, even though he wasn't looking, and joined him at the fire. Compliments from Shem would never get old. At least I could blame the heat of the fire for my rosy cheeks.

"You look for complicated solutions," I replied in a soft voice. "Usually our wants and desires are far more simple: Survival. Protection. Love."

The last word came out a bit breathy.

I averted my eyes to the Kathenoth that he still held. "In this case, the owner seems driven by fear. She made foolish decisions, and was forced to protect herself."

I could see it so clearly, because the owner might as well have been me.

Closing my eyes for a moment to hide the feelings that surged up, I tried—unsuccessfully—to push away what'd happened a few short months ago.

Unbidden, the memory of holding a small glass jar made my fingertips tingle, as if I were experiencing it now. As if it was just yesterday that Asher had threatened to reveal my secrets. In the heat of the moment, I'd used my shape-shifting Gift to turn him into a lizard on instinct. Forced into the awful choice to protect myself or lose everything, that choice had led to the same fate for the rest of my friends. A rash chain of events had followed. I still wondered if I could've stopped it somehow.

Blinking, I pasted a smile on my face as I met Shem's gaze.

"Is everything well?" Instead of his usual scholarly gaze focused on some internal thought, his piercing eyes were now pinned on my face, seeing more than I'd meant for him to.

I was tempted to tell him.

My desire to be honest with Shem grew each day that I spent in his presence. Biting my lip, I hesitated. I couldn't share such a terrible secret until I knew if I were truly special to him, or if he simply made everyone feel that way.

If I revealed that I was both a shape-shifter and

the reason for my friends' disappearances, he might never see me the same again.

I was terrified to take that risk.

Rejection would be the least of my problems, though. I'd also be forced to leave my new home in the castle. Depending on the severity of my offense, I'd end up in the dungeons, in servitude, or on the run. But worst of all, they'd undoubtedly sever my Gift and leave me to slowly deteriorate until the Severance caused me to give up on living.

I took a deep breath and released it. "Nothing important." I gave him a small smile. It was the best I could do.

"If something is bothering you, I hope you'll share with me," Shem tried again, not moving. The firelight flickered in his eyes, turning them into a pale blue fire of their own.

I considered it. *What if I told him the truth? What would he do?* There were too many unknowns. I'd paused too long to simply brush off his concerns though. "I'm just… thinking of my father."

A partial truth.

After all, when everything had happened, I *had* included my father. I'd abandoned him along with the rest of my friends in the human world. It was harder to regret that particular choice, after everything he'd done.

Shem didn't know that though. I'd led him to believe my father had abandoned me.

"I… wonder if he's thought of me at all in the last few months," I managed to say. Silently, I added to myself, *And if he's still alive…*

That seemed to satisfy Shem.

He placed a warm hand on my arm for a brief second before removing it. "Come," he said with a soft smile. "Let's go to dinner. The others will talk if we don't leave soon."

That was a perfect opportunity for me to ask, *Is there any truth to what they're saying?*

But he'd already turned to leave, taking hold of the door and swinging it open for me.

For the thousandth time, the moment had passed before I could catch it.

5

"LET'S TAKE A QUICK detour." Shem said, as he stepped into the hall and held up the Kathenoth. "I need to put this away." He stretched a hand out to me, indicating that he wanted to travel directly.

I accepted with a smile. "Where're we going?"

"Have you ever been to the vault for enchanted objects?" His fingers curled around mine. We both ignored the pointed look from Gabriel.

My excitement rose as I shook my head. I didn't even know where it was, and I'd explored most of the castle at this point.

THE SECRET SHADOW

"It's deep within the east wing, above the king and queen's private chambers," he said with a grin. That explained why I'd never seen it or heard of it. This side of the castle was heavily guarded and off-limits to most residents.

My sole visit to the east wing beyond Shem's council rooms had been in fly form, late at night. After dodging multiple guards, flying so hard my little heart nearly gave out, I'd decided it wasn't worth the risk to go back.

"If we hurry, we'll have time for a quick tour," he said now, with a squeeze of my fingers right before he traveled, taking me with him.

One second we stood in the bright light of the red carpeted hallway, and the next, we were in a similar hallway, but darker—there weren't any windows here. If Shem hadn't said it was above the royal chambers, I'd have guessed it to be the lowest level of the castle, instead of the highest. The air was hushed. As if no one came to this floor.

At one end of the hall stood a member of the Guard. Turning my head slowly, so as not to seem suspicious, I looked in the opposite direction.

Another guard.

Her eyes narrowed on my face, but with the prince there, she didn't say anything.

Shem nodded back, acknowledging her briefly, but he was focused on the dark blue door in front of us. The decorative black iron swirled over it creating a design that looked like dozens of thin snakes, woven together in intricate patterns from floor to ceiling. A soft vibration came from the metal. It seemed to expand and shift ever so slightly, almost as if the snakes were alive.

The vault door.

Shem touched the door handle. Without warning, two of the iron snakes uncoiled their heads and struck the prince's hand, wrapping tightly around his wrist, holding him firmly in place.

I hissed in surprise, but Shem didn't flinch.

If I had to guess, I'd say the iron was also spelled against travel. Quite an effective lock.

He waited patiently.

After a long pause, the iron unwound, slithering back into place with metallic scrapes.

The lock clicked open softly.

"It's enchanted to allow my family in, but all others need a key," Shem explained, as the door creaked open. He entered, still holding my hand.

I trailed behind him, blinking as my eyes adjusted to the dark room. There was only one

THE SECRET SHADOW

window at the back wall. It created a square of sunlight on the dark wood floor, but otherwise only dim light reached the shelves along the walls. Various tables filled the room, covered in objects, seemingly without rhyme or reason.

Shem lit a candle by the door. It caused a chain reaction spell until all the candles around the room were lit.

My eyes were immediately drawn to the opposite side of the room where an entire wall seemed to glitter.

Light bounced off of countless jewels—rings, earrings, necklaces, and even multiple crowns sat on carved wooden heads designed to display them. In the corner, a dress made of gems sparkled so brightly it made my eyes water. Rubies, emeralds, topaz, sapphire, diamonds, amethysts, onyx, and so many more, were all sewn into the lace. It must weigh more than any woman wearing it ever could, which most likely meant it was enchanted to carry itself.

"This is where we store all Kathenoths." Shem strode toward another shelf, running a hand along all the different bindings before placing the newest Kathenoth beside the others. I'd barely noticed the bookcase because it was so ordinary. But the shelves were full of journals in all shapes and sizes. Some seemed new, while others looked brittle and ancient, like they'd fall apart if anyone tried to read them now.

Turning away from the books with a shiver, I stepped further into the vault, trailing a hand along a nearby table. It had beautiful carvings all around the mahogany edges and a red velvet cloth on top. There were different display cases for every item.

"Each table holds enchanted objects that somewhat belong in the same category," Shem explained as he joined me.

A key, which didn't seem significant in any way, sat above a handwritten description with a looping cursive. *Enchanted to unlock any door in the world.*

My brows rose. That could be useful.

I slowly circled the table.

A knife... *enchanted to always hit the intended target.*

If someone had that, they'd never lose a fight.

Lifting my gaze, I spun in a slow circle taking in all the other tables with what must be hundreds of objects displayed. Most appeared simple at first glance, but each one came with an inscription for its usage: a lamp, a mirror, a spindle...

There was a magical quality to the air, almost a

heaviness. As if the history in these objects was making itself known.

"Feel free to look around." Shem waved a hand at all the tables. "This is the royal family collection. It's been built up over the centuries."

As I passed a mirror, I expected it to show my reflection, but it remained dark, nearly black. Uncomfortable, I didn't stop to read whatever enchantment made it that way, moving away from the enchanted objects instead. "Does anyone use them?"

Shem shrugged. "I'm sure they've all been used at some point. I've studied many of the objects in this room myself, but I still don't know half of them." He lifted the key I'd noticed before, then set it back in its stand gently, before drawing his finger over the spindle beside it. "Some of these were created by the crown for a specific purpose. Others were confiscated—sometimes before they could be used, but usually after."

I drew a shallow breath, feeling like I should whisper. "There's so many."

"Isn't it incredible?"

I nodded, hand hovering over the same table, too awed to risk actually touching anything. "Very."

"Well," he said, gesturing to the shelf of

Kathenoths. "Now that that's taken care of, time for dinner."

* * *

NORMALLY WHEN DINING with the prince in the evenings, I found myself competing for his attention with at least half a dozen council members. We rarely spoke. I could only hope it was because he didn't want to play favorites.

Today, however, we entered the dining hall together. I threw my shoulders back and lifted my chin, daring anyone to question it.

At the far end, a long table stood slightly raised for the royal family. It had a dozen extra seats for whichever honored guests they invited to join them. At their backs was an enormous window overlooking the entrance to the main gardens.

The nearest three tables were reserved for the three royal councils. Many more tables filled the large room for other castle residents and guests.

Shem often sat with his council instead of on the raised dais with his parents, especially when they weren't yet present or when he arrived late.

As we reached the council table, he pulled out a chair for me and took the one right beside it.

Over half of his council was still here. Some seemed nearly finished, but they immediately slowed upon Shem's arrival. My best guess was that they'd already dragged out their meal as much as possible. Others looked like they were just beginning. They'd probably circulated throughout the room making conversation, waiting for the prince to show.

Before I could think of something witty to say, Milcah immediately engaged Shem in conversation from across the table. "We were discussing some particularly juicy gossip about her Majesty's newest council member," she murmured, loud enough for us to hear, but not so loud that the unfamiliar woman seated at the queen's council table next to ours would overhear.

"Oh?" Shem replied politely, ever the gentleman. Queen Samaria frequently added to her council and had twice as many members as both the prince and King Jubal's councils put together. Her council table wasn't nearly large enough, so the members tended to rotate between their table, the dais when invited, and whatever open seating the main tables had available.

Since it was common for those on a council to travel for the crown—and in the queen's case to also remove council members on a regular basis—it was difficult to put an exact number on how many she had. But the queen was rumored to have hundreds in her employ.

"What're they saying?" I chimed in, determined not to be ignored.

Though Milcah's mouth curled slightly in distaste, she couldn't avoid a direct question. Still, when she answered, she focused on Shem, as if he were the one who'd asked. "Supposedly she has a strong Gift. Maybe even dangerous."

Servants slipped up to our table unobtrusively, placing the first course before the prince and I, filling our drinks. Because it was Shem, one of them also stayed close by along the wall.

Laban reached for his drink, swirling the dark liquid and gazing thoughtfully out at the gardens. "Perhaps a water-based Gift? Or fire?"

Those Gifts tended to cause the most accidents before the owner got them under control. The king was rumored to have the Gift of fire, though like all Jinn, he tended to keep his Gifts to himself.

Did they have a conversation like this about me when I first joined the council? I held back a shiver. I could only hope they'd been as far off base in their guesses then as they likely were now.

"I think we would've heard of the damage if it were something so obvious as that," Jerusha scoffed, smiling with her teeth bared.

Quirking a brow at Shem, who'd quietly picked up his silverware and begun to cut into the meat on his plate, I asked, "What do you think it might be?"

He set down the heavy silver knife, chewing thoughtfully. The nearby council members all tried to pretend they weren't hanging on his every word as they waited. "I do have to agree with Jerusha. A physical Gift would be fairly noticeable. It's likely more of an internal ability. Something they can use without others being aware of it."

"Such as?" *He means a Gift like mine. Is he going to say shape-shifting?*

A sensation unexpectedly swept over me, almost like being inside a bubble, where the voices around me dimmed and a cool wave washed over my skin.

A small part of me wanted him to say it, if only to know what his reaction to the idea might be. Would he abhor it? Or find it fascinating? Or something in-between?

"I don't know…" It seemed like he cut off for some reason. Then the bubble burst and everything rushed back into clear focus. I sucked in a steadying breath, taking a drink to hide my reaction.

Shem tapped his fingers against the table, considering. The candlelight in the center flickered across his face, highlighting the sharp angles of his cheekbones and jaw. "Perhaps another mind-reader?" He shook his head again at all the possibilities, though he didn't seem concerned—his mental defenses were likely ten times stronger than my own. More likely he was curious.

My shoulders relaxed.

Just last month, a young Jinni from a few islands over, a distant relative of the royal family, had inadvertently revealed a newly formed mind-reading Gift. She'd immediately been pressed into joining the Jinni Guard, with its many checks and balances.

If a Jinni from a powerful family refused an invitation to join the Jinni Guard, it could lead to being banned from Resh, our capital city, for good. All in the name of protecting the royal family, of course. Many Jinn were, in fact, banned from visiting this island due to possessing dangerous Gifts of some kind.

But I'd gathered through hints and whispers that others from less-influential families weren't always offered those options, and often ended up in the dungeons instead. For those who had no family ties to protect them at all, their Gift might be severed completely. It was rare and cruel, but it happened.

A Jinni seldom survived a Severance.

I shivered. Picking up my fork to mask the involuntary movement, I focused on my meal and tried not to think about my utter lack of connections, family or otherwise.

For the rest of the evening, I ignored the conversation swirling around me, not wanting to draw attention. Shem's eyes caught on mine briefly in silent question. I just smiled at him and took another bite.

He'd grown quieter as well, allowing the others to drive the discussion, providing short, simple answers when addressed directly. A few more times, he glanced my way. Both of us knew better than to have an intimate conversation here. But when a server came to refill our drinks, Shem faced him as if to ask a question, murmuring to me instead, "Is everything all right?"

Out of the corner of my eye, Milcah leaned forward a bit, so when I smiled softly and nodded, I pretended my response was to the server as well.

The thin Jinni kept a straight face as she lifted the water carafe and the towel that caught condensation. She was more than used to such things, moving on to refill the other council members drinks without skipping a beat.

Shem met my gaze and licked his lips, seeming to consider.

Before he could say anything, a hand landed on his shoulder. "Your highness."

"Josiah," Shem said, blowing out a breath, turning to face him. I noticed the younger guard was attempting to grow a straggly beard. The prince's face reflected oddly in Josiah's thick armor breastplate. "Is there an urgent matter?" A polite way of asking why he'd so rudely interrupted us during dinner.

I pretended not to listen while peeking over my shoulder at them. Josiah had pulled back his hand and stood at attention.

"Actually yes, your highness—" Josiah's frown landed on me briefly, before darting around the table, "—it is urgent. The castle has been placed on high alert."

Without being obvious, I used my drink as an excuse to turn, surveying the room as I took a sip. Where one guard usually stood near each table, now there were three. They weren't eating or even joining in the conversations. If anything, they eyed the familiar dinner guests with narrowed eyes.

My skin prickled.

Instinct told me something was wrong.

"I've been asked to bring you to the royal chambers immediately," Josiah continued.

The king and queen's rooms.

The heavy carpet gave a soft whoosh as Shem pushed back his chair and stood, folding his napkin and depositing it neatly beside his plate.

"Alone," Josiah added, as his eyes swung to mine once more.

I hadn't realized I'd stood.

I flushed.

Lowering myself back into the chair with grace, I pretended not to notice his disdain or the council members murmuring about my audacity.

"My apologies," Prince Shem said to the table, but his eyes stayed glued to mine. He wrinkled his nose in annoyance. "I'm sure it's nothing. I'll be back promptly." To the rest of the table, he added with a wave of his hand. "Please don't wait on ceremony, continue with your meal."

Nodding with the others, I stared at his back and watched his leather boots until they disappeared between tables, heading for the large doors at the dining hall entrance, where they would travel the remaining distance to the east side of the castle.

I softly let out the breath I'd been holding.

"Is there something we should know about?" Jerusha's loud voice drew everyone's attention back to me.

When I gave her a blank look, she waved in Shem's direction. "You seemed to believe you belonged in a high security meeting?"

Oh, *that*.

I flushed again and cleared my throat, taking a sip of water in a desperate attempt to buy time to think. "I'm afraid the guard misunderstood," I said lightly, careful not to blame Jerusha, or she'd dig in her heels. "I was about to go to the lavatory. The timing was coincidental." To prove it, I pushed back from the table and stood again. "The Guard is always trying to cause a spectacle. Thankfully, our *council* is above such things."

Before she could question me further, I slipped away from the table, keeping a casual pace until I reached one of the doors and exited the room. Once out of sight and away from the enchantments in the dining room that prevented travel, I immediately flashed away to a familiar, dark alcove near Shem's council rooms.

THE SECRET SHADOW

Something told me this crisis, whatever it was, would affect me. I needed to get closer so I could overhear.

Hidden away in the shadowy corner, I peeked out briefly to make sure I was alone, before shifting.

Small, smaller, and smaller still.

Tiny insect feet replaced my limbs.

Membrane-thin wings stretched out from my back.

My two eyes altered to become a few thousand on each side.

I was a fly on the wall.

Pushing off, I flapped my new wings with all my strength, racing toward the royal quarters.

As I passed the tightly closed door to their rooms, I shot down the hall and back, mind racing. *How do I get in?* I knew from experience and court gossip that the royal chambers didn't have many weaknesses. The outside windows were spelled even when open, so it wasn't possible to get in from outside. As far as the interior, the chambers had multiple doors, but they were all currently closed.

At the end of the hall, a meeting room frequently used by the king and queen was propped open. It wasn't connected to the rooms they used now... except, possibly, by some lavatory pipes between the bathing rooms...

I veered sharply toward it.

I can't believe I'm about to do this. Though I'd entertained the idea a few times before, I'd always dismissed it. I'd never been this desperate.

Inside the meeting room, I headed straight for the lavatory, where the yawning dark hole led to a series of pipes that eventually drained out of the castle.

Since I'd refused to stoop this low in the past, I could only hope it connected to the lavatory in the royal chambers as well.

Interesting.

The smells that would've disgusted me in human form seemed strangely normal. *This shape has some benefits.* Flying through the nearly pitch-black pipes, I hit an intersection that led straight ahead, as well as upward, and down. I followed my instincts.

Up.

Light appeared above.

I hurtled out of the disgusting pipes and into a fancy, tiled bathing room. I headed toward the connecting chambers—what I hoped were the *royal* chambers.

Voices grew louder as I flitted inside and landed

on the back of the first chair I could find. Slowly, I crawled with sticky insect legs along the fabric until I could peer over the edge.

Across the room, near the door, at least ten guards stood surrounding the king and queen. Two more guards stood at the entrance with Prince Shem. Captain Uriel joined them.

I rarely saw the captain of the Guard.

If he was there, it must be serious.

Prince Shem clearly had a similar thought. Frowning, he asked, "What's going on?"

"Sit with your mother," the king answered instead, waving him and Queen Samaria in my general direction. The queen lowered herself onto a warm green sofa nearby, small and fragile against the enormous furniture. Though her dress seemed to be a delicate silver silk at first glance, it was iridescent, reflecting a rainbow of colors beneath, whenever she moved.

Shaking his head, Shem gestured back toward the door. "I was in the middle of dinner. Couldn't this wait?"

"I'm afraid not, son." The king rubbed a hand across his wrinkled brow, turning to pace. The decorative chains on his heavy boots clinked with each step. "You need to be briefed by the guard. We must make some decisions immediately."

Frowning, Shem crossed the carpet to sit beside his mother. "Well then, by all means, begin."

Uriel cleared his throat. *Is he nervous?* I could understand a younger guard fidgeting under the pressure of speaking to the royal family, but not Uriel. My own anxiety level rose in anticipation.

"There's a threat in the castle, your highnesses," the captain began slowly, gripping the crystal spear at his side so tight his knuckles whitened. "We've discovered a shape-shifter."

My tiny insect heart nearly gave out.

They found me!

I took off flying before I even had a direction.

A wall rose up before me, and I had to veer right, spiraling wildly as I lost my balance in the air, barely slowing in time for a rough landing on the carpeted floor.

The queen had jumped up from the sofa. "We must evacuate immediately!"

Oh, don't worry, I'm already gone! I thought in a panic.

But my wings trembled so hard I couldn't fly.

The room spun.

Calm down, I berated myself. *They can't*

THE SECRET SHADOW

possibly know it's me. That thought sped up my racing heart to dangerous levels. *Do they?*

This was so unfair. Just when I'd been falling for the prince, I had to lose him too. Now I'd have to run before they caught me.

Perhaps they were already searching my rooms.

I should try to learn as much as I can about their plans to catch me before I sneak out. Logical thinking didn't help my nerves at all.

The queen swayed slightly. Prince Shem stood to put an arm around her. "What do you mean a shape-shifter? Is it truly in the castle? How did it get past the guards at the first and second gate? Or the entrance? Are you certain?"

It? I rolled my many eyes at his ignorance, but his last question caught my attention. *Yes, are you certain?* I fluttered my wings, hopeful. *Maybe they don't know for sure.*

Even as I thought this, I sagged in defeat. It didn't matter if they knew for sure or not. Now that they were on the alert, it was only a matter of time. *I still have to go.* I focused on calming down enough to fly out the way I'd come in.

The king stopped pacing, coming to put a hand on his son's shoulder. "Unfortunately, my son, we have proof."

The queen sank onto the green cushions, shuddering, as if she couldn't hold herself up any longer.

My bug eyes would've widened if they could have. *Did I slip? When?*

"A serving woman by the name of Hila approached the head of staff in his office less than an hour ago, inquiring after new guests and employees in the castle."

But… I didn't do that.

If I could've shaken my head, I would have.

The shifter wasn't me.

For one thing, I didn't like to shift into another Jinni, whether known or unknown. Not after what'd happened with Asher. More importantly, it was far too risky.

Creeping along the floor on all six legs, I tried to get closer.

"I fail to see how that would raise an alarm?" Shem was saying to both his father and the guards.

"Hila hasn't been employed by the castle in over a decade," Uriel said in a flat tone. "Not since she died."

My chest grew tight.

"Ah," the prince said, absently lowering himself

to sit beside his mother, dragging out the word as he slumped back against the sofa. "I see."

So did I. *It's hard to argue with that evidence.*

For once, the Jinni Guard was right.

There was another shape-shifter in the castle.

6

THE QUEEN PALED AT the revelation. "Why didn't the head of staff apprehend this shifter right then and there?"

That would've certainly made my life easier. The many eyes of my fly form were giving me a severe headache. My wings finally felt steady enough to fly, but now I couldn't leave without gathering more information.

I flew up to the mantle for a better view, landing behind a small statue set of the royal family, peering out from behind a miniature, marble Shem.

"He assumed that this shifter was more dangerous than it appeared," the king took over the explanation for the guard, whose shoulders slumped slightly in relief. "And rightly so."

There they go calling the shifter an "it" again. I itched to get away from this anxious hatred of my kind, but hearing the details was more important than my comfort right now.

The king strode to sit beside the queen as well, taking her hand. "Fortunately for us, the head of staff was clever. He made excuses to the shifter about needing a different ledger to get the information she needed, and if she would wait in his office, he would fetch it."

When the king waved toward the guards, I flinched automatically. *They don't know I'm here,* I reminded myself.

"The head of staff instantly summoned Captain Uriel," the king continued. "And half the Guard closed in on the room." He stood again to pace, gesturing for Uriel to continue the story.

I crept out from behind the little statue of the prince, forgetting myself, wanting to lecture them. *If this other shifter wanted to hurt you, you'd never have had a chance.* Scoffing, I added to myself, *You don't think like a shifter or you'd have searched this room much more carefully.* They could get wise at any moment though. I pulled back out of sight once more.

Uriel stepped forward. "The shifter must've known she'd been discovered. When we entered the head of staff's office, she attacked the first guard in lion form, forcing her way out of the room and tearing down the hall. By the time we'd rounded the corner, the shifter was gone."

Impressive. Whoever she is, she's fast. I'd picked up speed over the last few months, but if that'd been me, they would've caught me mid-shift for sure.

"Most likely this shifter went to the first window they could find," Shem's voice lifted, almost hopeful, as he turned to his father. "Surely they wanted to vacate the premises straightaway."

Agreed. People underestimated Prince Shem because his head was so often in the clouds, but he was more perceptive than most realized.

"Not possible." Uriel shook his head, bringing his hands behind his back, standing stiffly. "When the head of staff alerted us to the danger, we immediately enacted the castle defense enchantments."

THE SECRET SHADOW

My tiny lungs couldn't seem to suck in enough air. I hadn't heard of any defenses that prevented someone from fleeing. That didn't bode well for me at all.

"They fell into place before we reached the office, less than an hour ago," he continued.

Was *that* what I'd experienced earlier when I'd felt that sensation like a bubble bursting around me? It'd been so subtle I hadn't recognized the hint of magic sweeping over me, but looking back it was perfectly clear.

"All inhabitants are currently locked inside the castle walls until the spell is lifted," Uriel finished. "Which also means we're trapped here. With the shifter."

My tiny stomach—or were there multiple stomachs?—curdled in a split second. Could a fly throw up? I was about to find out…

I'm trapped.

I couldn't leave even if I wanted to. Everything in me wanted to test the spell by flying through the nearest window here and now.

Don't do anything foolish.

If I set off the enchantment and alerted the Jinni Guard to my presence, there'd be no escape.

"Shouldn't we lift it to allow the Guard to get

you and mother to safety?" Shem asked, frowning.

Queen Samaria lifted a shaking hand to her forehead. "I quite agree."

"The enchantment won't be lifted. Not until the shifter is caught." King Jubal cut a hand through the air with finality. "It's too risky. If we allow the shifter the chance to escape, we'd give them free reign of the kingdom. They could attack at any time. We would be in even more danger if we let it loose, than we are now."

All the little hairs along my tiny body lifted as his words sunk in. *They're not going to stop until they find a shifter. Any shifter. Whether it's the one who caused this uproar or not.*

This other shifter clearly knew more about their Gift than I did. They probably knew exactly what the Guard would do in a situation like this and would be prepared. Which meant they weren't likely to get caught.

That led to an even worse realization.

They're not going to catch the intruder… They're going to catch me.

7

"I HATE THIS," SHEM said.

Silently, I agreed with him.

"Don't fear, your majesties," Captain Uriel reassured the royal family. "Even now we already have measures in place that will help us catch the shifter." He gestured vaguely. I tensed. What measures? How could I avoid capture if I didn't recognize the trap?

Off the top of my head, there was only one Gift I could think of that might discover a shape-shifter: mind-reading. Was Captain Uriel a mind-reader? Or one of his guards?

Creeping back, I let the little statue of the prince block my tiny body from view. I checked my mental walls, and then built them even higher.

Unless a Gift was exceptional, even a powerful mind-reader usually needed to focus on a subject to hear their thoughts, but that was the extent of my knowledge—I didn't know if "focus" meant an intentional stare or if a passing glance at a seemingly-innocent fly in the room would spell my doom. When it came to the Guard members, chosen for the strength of their abilities, it wasn't worth the risk.

"What do you think the shifter is after?" Shem asked, ignoring Uriel's attempt to placate them. "How do you know they're even a threat?"

King Jubal scoffed. "*All* shifters are a threat. They could replace any one of us in a heartbeat—and if they were smart, no one would be the wiser. No other Gift is more dangerous to us. Use your head, boy."

Shem flushed, but his mother put a soothing hand on his arm and added, "We wouldn't expect you to have considered all the angles, dear. You've never faced a shifter before. But your father and I had an unfortunate encounter, many years ago. The danger is quite real."

My heart stuttered.

My mother had been a shifter—could they be talking about her? After all, she'd been in their Guard. I'd always wondered why she'd left so suddenly…

Shem paled. "You think they'd replace *you*." It wasn't a question.

A heavy pause filled the room.

"They could take anyone's place, really," Captain Uriel dared to re-enter the tense conversation. "We developed a rough plan the last time we were in this situation… There's a spell that can leave an invisible mark on a Jinni—one that a shifter couldn't possibly replicate, as they cannot see it."

"Ah yes," Queen Samaria's face lifted, and she sucked in a hopeful breath. "The mark. It doesn't fade for weeks. We'll need to begin interrogations at once."

"Interrogations?" Shem frowned at his parents.

His father stared into the thick carpet, lost in thought.

Captain Uriel glanced at the king, who remained silent, before he cleared his throat and said, "We will determine with one hundred percent certainty that a

Jinni is who they claim to be, before giving them the mark. If we make our way through the castle this way, in theory, we could complete the interrogations by the second day. Or the third at the very latest."

"Perhaps we could call it an 'interview' instead?" Shem suggested, running a hand through his hair and wincing. "They're not going to like it."

"They don't have to like it," King Jubal declared in a sharp tone that made me flinch. I hadn't thought he was listening. "They'll do what their king and queen demand."

"We have full confidence we'll catch the shifter," Captain Uriel inserted before Shem could protest further, turning to the queen with a smile. "Most likely within the day."

She smiled back, shoulders relaxing.

My wings vibrated with renewed panic.

My chances at a full life here with Prince Shem were absolutely and without a doubt over.

Without connections or family in power like the other council members, if I was caught I'd spend the rest of my life in the dungeons below. That wouldn't last long though, since they'd probably punish me with a Severance as well. If my Gift was severed, my remaining days would be few.

THE SECRET SHADOW

Slowly, staying out of sight as much as possible, I used the sticky pads on my tiny feet to crawl down the wall to the thick, patterned carpet, heading as quickly as I could in such a tiny form toward the bathing room: my escape.

It was time to find a way out of the castle.

At some silent signal, the guards began to spread out across the room.

I tucked myself behind the leg of a chair. Burrowing into the carpet, I waited for the nearest guard to pass by. As he headed for the lavatory, the queen followed in his wake, waiting for him to pronounce it safe.

She closed the door on his heels as soon as he did so. My heart sank.

My only exit was barred.

I managed to stay ahead of the guard searching my section of the room. When he paused to respond to the king, I quickly flew behind him. Whether or not they could sense me, I didn't want to stay and find out.

I need to get out of here. Now. Every second I stuck around, I was asking to be caught.

Flinging out my wings, I took a risk.

I flew straight up to the ceiling—the least likely place they'd look. Once there, I flew horizontal along the surface, so hard my little heart almost exploded.

Upside down, I landed. All my eyes were trained on the Jinn below me. After a second to catch my breath, I pushed off, aiming for the entrance.

Dropping onto the tiny ledge above the double doors, I pressed against the wood. From this height, I shouldn't be noticed.

For good measure, though, I flipped onto my back, feet in the air. *Play dead.*

While I impatiently waited for the guards to finish their search and open the door below, I tried to calm my beating heart. If I listened for helpful information, maybe they'd give me a clue on how to survive this.

"The royal chambers are safe, your majesties," the youngest Jinni guard finally said with a bow. "We've searched every room thoroughly, both before and after your arrival. We recommend you remain here while we begin our search throughout the rest of the castle."

"Apologies." Shem stood from where he'd waited on the sofa. He wasn't apologetic at all. "I'm afraid I can't do that. I can't in good conscience leave my council members unaware and unprotected."

King Jubal held out a hand, barring Shem from

moving toward the door. "You must tell no one."

Fists clenched at his sides, Shem sidestepped the king. "I have to warn them."

With a flick of the king's hand, four members of the Guard fell into position in front of the double doors, spears crossed.

"Father," Shem snapped, turning around. From my vantage point, I could only see the top of his head.

King Jubal crossed his arms. "We cannot lose the element of surprise," his voice overrode whatever Shem had been about to say, unyielding.

"What surprise?" Shem scoffed. "The shifter ran from our guards. They most likely tried to escape shortly after and have already discovered the enchantments that hold them prisoner in these walls."

Did that mean the enchantments didn't include a trap when tested? I wouldn't risk trying it yet, but that was a tiny ray of light.

"There's no *element of surprise*," Shem continued, advancing toward his father slowly, stopping in front of him. "They *know* we're looking for them."

His father said nothing, expressionless, as if he wouldn't back down now, even if it did appear foolish.

Shem visibly took a deep breath, ignoring the guards. Focusing on his father, he murmured, "Let me warn my council. They deserve to know." Another pause, and he added, "The court will piece together that there's a threat once the interviews begin anyway."

Grunting, King Jubal relented and nodded to the guards. "Just wait long enough to get the mark before you go."

"How long will that take?" Shem glanced between his father and Uriel.

The captain cleared his throat. "It's a complicated spell. Hopefully within the next hour we'll have gathered everything we need."

"A lot can happen in an hour. I need to warn them. You can give me the mark when I get back." Shem stepped up to the four guards blocking the door, waiting impatiently for them to step aside and open it.

"Son—" the king cut off, darting a look at Queen Samaria as if asking her to intervene.

She merely shrugged. "He's with his guards. And the shifter isn't going to attack them in a crowded dining hall full of powerful Jinn. Let him do

THE SECRET SHADOW

what he needs to do. He'll be back shortly."

Shem strode through the door before she'd finished speaking, flanked by two guards rushing to keep up. As soon as they stepped past the enchantments that prevented travel, they vanished.

My racing heart picked up speed again. This was my chance to escape the room as well.

All eyes were on the door below.

I couldn't fly through the exit without risking being seen.

The guards were closing the doors behind the prince. In a few seconds, I'd be locked in once more. This was my only chance.

This is insane.

I *should* stay put. Wait here in the *one room* in the entire castle that they'd pronounced shifter-free, where I could be confident that I wouldn't be caught. Where I could wait it out.

If nothing else, I certainly *shouldn't* put myself directly in the guards' line of sight.

The king turned to speak with Uriel, and the queen's eyes latched onto them as well. Below, two of the four guards at the door had already taken up position with their backs to it, and the remaining two weren't looking up. If I remained above eye level, I might make it through unseen.

It was now or never.

The crack between the door and the frame was narrowing.

With only a few fingers of space left, I leapt off the ledge and flew through the door, nearly clipping my wings as the heavy wood thudded closed behind me.

Shem was already gone, of course. The hall was empty.

On instinct, I tried to travel too. The most common Gift in Jinn was traveling from one distant place to another, and I had just as much range as the prince, if not a little bit more. I swore silently as nothing happened—I'd learned very early on that I couldn't travel while in animal form, but I used the Gift so often it became muscle memory and I sometimes forgot.

Shem and his guards would've already arrived at the dining hall entrance.

If I didn't follow suit shortly, he might come looking for me. He wanted to warn his entire council after all.

My absence would be highly suspicious behavior at the absolute worst time.

It was too late to pretend I'd never left the dining

hall, but I could still get back before he finished warning the others.

I pushed my tiny wings to their limits. Heading down the empty hall, I searched for a safe place to shift back into my true form.

A Jinni with dark eyebrows and graying hair passed by below me, heading in the opposite direction. I nearly grazed the high ceiling in my attempts to hide from him. He never looked up.

At the sight of an open tea room down the hall, I changed direction.

I circled the room, still near the ceiling tiles, trying to capture every angle through my bug eyes.

It appeared empty.

I dropped onto the table in the center, landing on a teapot—it was cold.

No one was here.

It still felt too exposed.

Pushing through my exhaustion, I forced my wings to carry me to a hidden space behind a lounge chair.

I shifted.

After straining so hard in my fly form, returning to my true self took the last of my energy. The transition was sharp. It felt like yanking off a piece of clothing so roughly that it ripped out bits of hair and scraped against tender skin.

My weakness wouldn't be noticeable to anyone else, but I could hardly stand.

I leaned against the back of the chair. For a long minute, I simply breathed in and out, eyes closed, and tried not to faint. I needed food and rest as soon as possible to regain my strength.

One problem at a time.

Right now, my secrets still remained my own. If I wanted it to stay that way, I needed to calmly return to finish my meal and act as if nothing had changed.

Bones aching, I stood and forced myself to travel to the dining hall entrance.

Exhaustion made me stagger as I materialized.

Prince Shem's voice floated toward me from within. "All council members please report for an emergency meeting."

Still breathing hard, I gulped a few deep breaths to steady myself before I wove back through the tables toward him. His back was to me, as he spoke to our table, "I'll explain more once we're all together. Please spread the word and make sure everyone is gathered in my chambers within a quarter hour."

Though their faces held questions, none of the

council members challenged his request, nodding before they strode out into the hallway and disappeared. Milcah's gaze caught mine briefly as the hall door was closing, before she vanished as well.

Smoothing out my face, I shoved my terror deep down, until I could almost pretend it didn't exist. I casually approached the table, touching Shem's arm lightly.

He flinched. It was almost imperceptible. When he turned to face me, he was calm, but there was more under the surface than he was letting on. "Jezebel," he said on a breath, seeming to relax slightly. "I was worried you'd gone off alone."

Pretending confusion took every bit of my willpower. "Why shouldn't I be alone?"

I tried to memorize his face without being obvious. That way I could take a piece of him with me when I left. The thought made me want to cry. I crossed my arms and bit the inside of my cheek to hide the rush of emotions.

He stared back, not moving, as if he wanted to tell me right then and there, despite the rest of the dining crowd listening in.

His guards stood on each side, and one of them shifted on his feet, breaking the spell between us.

"This isn't a good place to share." He ran a frustrated hand through his hair, glancing at the guards again. "I've called an urgent council meeting. Please go join the others, and I'll explain everything shortly."

I obeyed, traveling to the hall outside his council chambers, arriving at the same time as a few others.

There were two guards outside his rooms now, instead of one. I slipped in on the heels of another circle, not giving either guard a chance to protest.

Once I snuck inside, I sank into a chair against the wall, partially hidden in the corner. I ignored the gossip buzzing around the room and closed my eyes to prevent anyone from trying to speak to me.

When Shem arrived, he strode in with a grim look. He didn't stand on ceremony, beginning his announcement right away, "The castle—and perhaps the royal family in particular—is very likely under attack."

He continued on ruthlessly over the gasps across the room. "I have it on good authority that we have a shape-shifter in our midst."

Now he did pause, allowing that to sink in.

Utter silence met his announcement, as we eyed those around us.

"I must ask that you keep this information to

yourselves, as we are trying to avoid a widespread panic in the castle while we search for the shifter."

He briefly explained the enchantment over the castle locking all of us in with this shifter, but he didn't say anything I didn't already know.

"I trust each of you know how to handle yourselves in this situation," Shem continued. "But I would also recommend that you begin a habit of traveling in groups, as well as bringing up your history with each other whenever you meet, as a precaution."

To check if you're speaking to a shape-shifter, he meant.

I swallowed hard. That would be effective.

It might also give me the slightest edge over this other shifter. They might have some knowledge of the castle, but if their shifting into an old staff member was any indication, their information was at least a decade old, if not more.

I, on the other hand, knew most of these council members personally. And they knew me, whether they wanted to admit it or not.

Shem rubbed his brow, as if a headache plagued him. "I'm afraid I'm duty-bound not to share further details at this time. Please return to your regular activities. Once I'm able to say more, you'll be the first to know."

The dismissal was clear. Council members slowly trickled out of the room in pairs or larger groups, as Shem had suggested, until only the prince was left.

And me.

I hadn't meant to stay behind, but my legs wobbled slightly beneath my dress, not ready to carry me anywhere just yet. "I'm sorry," I whispered when his gaze found me in the corner. "I need a moment."

He misunderstood. "I should be the one to apologize," he said, striding to sit on the sofa across from me, leaning on his knees so that only a small space separated us. "It's my fault you're in this situation. If I hadn't asked you to stay at the castle, you wouldn't be in any danger."

"There's always danger in Jinn," I said with a soft laugh, waving off his worries.

"That may be so." He remained serious, reaching a hand toward mine. "But I still fear for your safety."

Swallowing the lump that brought to my throat, I looked away from his earnest eyes and down at his hand where it covered my own. Though I wanted to respond in kind, I froze. "I don't suppose there's a way I could avoid this awful business altogether?" I finally managed to say, trying to keep my voice light.

He squeezed my fingers. "I'm afraid not."

I'd assumed as much. I shouldn't push him to tell me anything else, no matter how desperately I wanted to know what the Guard was planning.

He wants me to ask questions, I told myself. *Otherwise he would've asked me to leave.*

I met his eyes and placed my other hand over his, not daring even to blink as I whispered, "Please... if there's anything else, you'd tell me, wouldn't you?"

"Yes..." he whispered back, uneasy, but not looking away, almost as if trapped by my gaze.

"Please?"

He gave in unexpectedly. "They're going to question every single resident in the castle."

The interviews.

Some sort of one-on-one examination.

It went unsaid that the Jinni Guard would be using *all* their resources during these polite interrogations, including every available spell and Gift.

I bit my lip.

Ducking my head, I sucked in a breath.

For a split second, I considered telling him the

truth. If he heard it from my lips, would he believe me? *Shem, I have to tell you, I'm a shifter... But not the one you're looking for, I swear.*

I shook my head, rubbing my forehead with my free hand.

Put it like that, and I don't even believe myself.

"What's wrong?" Shem responded by moving from the sofa to a chair right next to mine, ducking down a bit, trying to catch my gaze.

As I lifted my eyes, a movement caught my attention in the balcony above. Milcah stood in the shadows. She'd never left. My heart rate doubled at the realization I'd almost spilled my secrets in front of her.

When she saw I'd spotted her, she stepped forward to lean casually on the balcony railing, eavesdropping without shame.

I was at a loss for words.

I pulled my hand from Shem's without thinking. It fluttered around like a bird without a perch, lighting on my hair, my earrings, my lap, and up again.

I couldn't tell him. Clearly.

Even if Milcah wasn't here, I knew better than to trust anyone with my secrets.

Shem's frown grew deeper the longer I was silent. "Jezebel, whatever it is, you can tell me."

I fiddled with my hair, tucking stray pieces back beneath my decorative headband. "You know the Guard makes me uncomfortable," I said slowly, searching for something I could tell him *and* Milcah at the same time, since she showed no signs of leaving.

Shem sat back in his chair and sighed. "I do. Your first few weeks here were an adjustment period to life in the castle… The Guard should've been more understanding of that. But what does that have to do with the shifter and the interviews?"

"I just…" I hesitated, then decided to simply tell the truth. Or part of it. "I'm not the shifter they're looking for, Shem. I'd rather not deal with them at all, if I didn't have to."

"They'll be completely professional," he assured me, brows drawing together in sympathy. "I wish I could allow you to keep your distance, truly. But you have nothing to worry about. They're only doing their job."

He's not going to bend.

Casting around for the next best solution, I leaned forward to take his hand again, despite Milcah's presence—or maybe I was daring *because* she was watching.

I swallowed hard before I could meet his eyes and speak, "Would you consider another favor then?"

Nodding, he held my gaze, absently stroking my hand.

"Can you tell them to interview me last?" I rushed to explain, "That way I'll never have need to speak with them."

"Oh? How so?"

I twisted my mouth into a semblance of a smile, hoping it seemed genuine. "I'm sure they'll find this dangerous shifter long before it's my turn for an interview."

The excuse sounded weak.

If he had any reason to suspect me now, he'd likely have me go first instead. Asking for this had been a mistake.

Yet, after a short pause, he nodded again in agreement. "I'll see what I can do."

My eyes widened. Normally he didn't like to give individual council members any special treatment. *Does that mean...* My traitorous heart soaked up the moment despite my fears. *Maybe he does feel something for me. Why else would he agree so quickly?*

"May I also request the same favor, your highness?" Milcah's voice floated over to us as she gracefully descended the stairs from the balcony. "I did not mean to overhear," she lied blatantly with wide eyes. "But I would ask that you might extend the same favor to myself and the rest of the council. Perhaps even in order of seniority?"

I glowered at her. That would move me from the last interview right back to the somewhere near the top of the list, and she knew it.

Politics in Jinn dictated that Shem always consider his council's wishes, so he murmured in agreement, trapped by the request as much as I was.

After Milcah thanked him, she stood over us for a few moments as the awkwardness grew.

"Well," Shem said, standing. "I suppose I should go make the request to the Guard."

We followed him out into the hall and the door clicked softly closed behind us.

"Wait!" I grabbed his hand once more to catch him before he traveled away. Milcah paused as well, but I gave her my shoulder and a brief, impatient glance over it to make it clear that this didn't include her.

With a barely contained huff, she turned on her

heel and traveled away.

Once she was gone, I turned back to Shem and bit my lip hopefully, knowing I was about to ask a lot. His fingers were warm in mine. "Don't tell the Guard that I was the one who asked? I don't want to give them another reason to dislike me."

Once again, he surprised me by agreeing immediately. "Of course. Don't worry over the Guard, Jezebel. You're safe here." Cupping a hand over my cheek, he smiled. "I'm sure they'll find the shifter within the next few hours. In the meantime, stay in your room and lock the door, just to be safe."

"I will," I agreed on a breath of relief. But it was short lived. I'd only bought myself a short delay. The Guard was still coming.

Shem gave my fingers a gentle squeeze, then let go.

He vanished.

I traveled as well, heading to my room as he'd asked.

While I didn't fear the shifter the way the others did, that didn't mean I wanted to get caught roaming the halls. That might seem suspicious.

Unlocking the door, I entered my room with a sigh. I'd remain here for now.

I didn't really have a choice, since I couldn't escape the castle, and I couldn't avoid the interview. My time was running out.

Unless... what if I found the other shifter and turned them in, before the Guard ever got close to me?

It was half a plan, but at least it was something.

I'd find a way to catch this other shifter myself.

8

THE SMALL CLOCK ON my desk ticked softly, counting down the hours until the Guard would discover my secret, sever my abilities, and send me to the dungeons for the rest of my short, Gift-less life. Not a single acceptable strategy for catching the shifter had come to me.

The empty glass jar on the desk beside the clock reminded me of the awful choices I'd made in the past when pressed into a corner.

I didn't want to hurt anyone this time.

Especially not Shem.

Crossing my arms, I paced between the window and the door, feeling a pressure building up behind my eyes.

If I couldn't find a third solution, he'd suffer either way: he'd either discover my secret or find that I'd disappeared without a goodbye.

It'd been at least a couple hours since dinner and the emergency council meeting. The Guard could arrive any minute. Being exposed as a shifter was simply not an option.

Time to test this enchantment.

It was designed to keep Jinn in, but maybe it would allow an animal to pass through... Only one way to find out.

Biting my lip, I unlatched the window, pulling it inward to open. It was better for everyone, including Shem, that the truth remained hidden.

Shifting into my favorite form, I became a little green lizard. It came to me easily now. I crawled up the wall to the window. My scaley sides expanded in a deep breath.

Smack.

I hit an invisible wall.

It knocked me backward.

Dizzy, I shifted even smaller, into a tiny flea. I crept toward the open window, more tentative this time.

The enchantment threw me back again.

Oof.

That hurt.

I couldn't leave, even in animal form.

Unfortunately, I'd half-expected it.

That crossed my last remaining option off my list.

Though it was extra work to shift back into my own form, I did so anyway, because I desperately needed to cry.

I flung myself across the middle of my bed and let the tears flow.

Gradually the ticking clock reminded me that nothing had changed. I was still on a deadline.

Tracing the decorative carvings on the bed post, I tried to focus on finding another way out of this.

My stomach growled.

It always begged me to eat after expending so much energy shifting.

I rang a little bell that would sound in the kitchens.

While I waited impatiently for someone on staff to answer my summons, I shifted one of my fingers into a talon and began carving into the thick bed post, between a design of two dragons that wrapped around it. If I dug deep enough, I could create a thin

THE SECRET SHADOW

but prominent shelf to place my first Kathenoth. Shem could find it and hopefully think someone had put a spell on me. Or maybe, if I was sure I could escape, I might write the truth…

My eyes caught on the glass jar on my desk. If I had a Kathenoth, would it include that story?

I flipped onto my back so I wouldn't see the jar anymore.

I'd have to write a Kathenoth for it to be found, and I didn't have the words.

Not even one.

Dragging my dark thoughts away from their hopeless spiral, I forced my attention to the shifter problem.

I imagined somehow trapping the intruder myself, bringing them before the king and queen as a hero, and watching them lift the castle enchantments without ever discovering my secrets. In that scenario, I could stay here, free and happy, with Shem.

I chewed on my bottom lip.

How will I even track them down, much less detain them, if they don't want to be found?

I wouldn't recognize the other shape-shifter unless they used their abilities right in front of me.

I need to make them use it.

This was where I'd been stumped for hours.

Meanwhile, every available member in the *entire* Jinni Guard—one thousand of the crown's most trusted and elite servants in the entire kingdom, at least half of whom lived here in the castle—were interviewing the occupants of the castle right now, at what I could only assume was a breakneck speed.

Shem had promised to do what he could, but at any moment they'd knock on my door. Perhaps they'd force me to use all my Gifts? Or maybe, the interview would be simpler than that. All they needed to ruin me was a truth spell.

Then, I would betray myself.

My stomach was hollow. I couldn't tell if it was from fear or hunger pains.

No one from the kitchens had answered. It'd been over an hour. Maybe the king and queen had given them a curfew. Either way, it looked like I wouldn't get anything to eat tonight.

Ignoring the pinching in my stomach, I climbed off the bed and paced to the window. Below, the luscious royal gardens sprawled out as far as the eye could see, with intricate paths between the different flora and fauna, and an enormous fountain in the middle. Normally, at least a few dozen Jinn strolled the footpaths at any time of day—even any time of night.

Now, though, it was empty.

Thanks to the barrier placed over the castle by the still unknown enchantment, it would remain that way until the shifter was caught.

Two days, the captain had said. *Three at most.*

Had any castle residences been caught outside the perimeter of the spell? They would've been left to puzzle out what happened on their own.

News of the enchantment would spread fast inside the castle though. They might not know *why* the castle was locked down, but it wasn't the first time the royal family had been under attack, and it wouldn't be the last. Most castle residents would take the temporary imprisonment in stride. I wondered if they'd feel the same way about these so-called "interviews."

Shem wanted us to remain in our rooms until it was our turn to speak with the Guard, but I'd lose my mind being locked up like this.

Every bone in my body wanted to do *something*.

I shook my head. Most likely there were guards in the hall.

Leaving would look suspicious.

My eyes drifted to the unassuming wardrobe in

the corner, and my lips twisted up.

Thank goodness for Shem and his loophole spell.

I crossed the room and placed a hand on the delicate, dark wood. It begged me to use it. I could sneak into the kitchens and feed myself. At the thought, my stomach growled again. I pressed a hand to my belly.

Inhaling deeply, I sighed.

There might still be staff in the kitchens, preparing for breakfast tomorrow.

"Soon," I whispered to myself. I'd wait until the middle of the night. "Just a few more hours."

As I paced, my eyes continued to flit back to the wardrobe.

The loophole spell worked two ways, after all.

Someone could also visit, *if* they wanted to.

A small part of me that I refused to acknowledge hoped that Shem might use it to come to me.

Another, more realistic part knew he had dozens of princely duties with this shifter situation keeping him busy—especially now that his father was preparing him to be king. Facing constant threats such as this would become his job soon enough. Even if that wasn't the case, he wasn't obligated to check

THE SECRET SHADOW

on me. There were a thousand reasons I shouldn't expect him. But I couldn't stop myself from hoping.

As the midnight bells rang, a shadow crossed beneath my doorway in the dimly lit hall.

I held my breath.

The shape continued on without stopping.

It was probably a guard on rotation.

I finally acknowledged the sharp pang of disappointment.

Shem wasn't coming.

The Guard hasn't come either, I reminded myself. *They would've started here first, if not for Shem requesting them not to. That has to mean something...*

Milcah might've requested the same favor, but he'd seemed more invested when he'd promised it to me. *Hadn't he?* My mind would drive me in circles if I let it.

Were the servants still in the kitchen? I should wait another hour... I paced away from the wardrobe and back to the window. At this rate, I'd create a groove in the floor.

On a normal night, I'd have traveled to the kitchens right after dinner. It was easy enough to find a staff member who didn't know I'd already eaten and request a meal tray be delivered to my room.

Whenever I practiced shifting, I did this out of necessity. I'd learned the hard way that if I strained my Gift too far without feeding it and getting rest, my body would betray me. Once, I'd collapsed in front of Shem. He'd worried for days.

An invisible hand grabbed my insides and twisted painfully as my stomach gurgled.

I needed to eat more than the half-dinner I'd had hours earlier.

Taking a deep breath in and out, I closed my eyes.

Just a little longer.

My feet moved on their own, returning me to the wardrobe. Again, I dragged myself away.

Only a shifter would show up demanding food right now. The kitchens will be empty soon.

If another hour could be considered soon.

My body stiffened. I stopped so abruptly that I nearly tripped over my own feet.

Whirling around, I stared at the wardrobe.

I know exactly how to find the shifter.

A little laugh escaped. I instantly felt lighter. The answer was so obvious I couldn't believe it hadn't occurred to me sooner.

While the Jinni Guard wasted time on their

THE SECRET SHADOW

precious interviews, all I needed to do was sneak into the kitchens and wait. The intruder had shifted as much as I had, maybe more. If they'd stayed hidden since their encounter, they wouldn't have had anything to eat since this afternoon.

Unless they had a stash somewhere, they were probably exhausted and growing desperate. There was only one place they could go.

I'll find them in the kitchen.

9

A KNOCK SOUNDED ON my door.

Shem came after all!

I dashed across the room to let him in, throwing on my robe so it'd look like I'd been sleeping. When I swung the door open, it wasn't the prince.

It was Gabriel.

A second Jinni Guard that I didn't recognize stood behind him.

"Can I help you?" I asked in an icy tone. Only my ability to shift my features kept the flush of fear from reaching my cheeks. Slowing my breathing was

THE SECRET SHADOW

much harder, but I concentrated my efforts on not giving away how frightened I was.

Gabriel spoke in a monotone as if repeating something he'd said a few dozen times already. "By order of the king, the Jinni Guard is appointed to speak with all castle inhabitants." He stepped forward, waving for the other guard to follow. "We are to conduct an interview focused on Gift—"

"Wait!" I put my hand on the door and pushed back, glaring. "You can't force your way into my room without asking!"

"Castle safety overrides privacy in this instance," Gabriel replied, meeting my gaze with a dark smile, as if he knew I was supposed to have more time, but was choosing to ignore it.

My heart pumped like I was facing a Lacklore instead of one of my least favorite castle acquaintances.

If I took this interview, I would fail.

Keeping my hand pressed firmly against the door, I lowered my voice, hoping it wouldn't shake. "Prince Shem didn't speak with you? He gave me—and the rest of his council—special status for the interviews. We're to go last, as we have too much work to do right now for us to waste our time on this."

"I'm afraid I don't know what you're referring to," he replied.

I didn't believe him for a second. His narrowed eyes hadn't blinked. "You're one of the newer residents in the castle," he added, as if that explained his decision.

My newness shouldn't affect whether I was the shifter or not in the slightest.

It simply made him more suspicious.

I let out a sigh, clutching my robe together at the neck. "You've roused me from bed without even checking the order of the interviews? I was *clearly* moved to the bottom of the list. I think the prince would find it highly disrespectful to hear you're disregarding his request."

Had Shem actually made the change? I had no idea.

I took a chance and began to swing the door shut as if the matter were already resolved.

Gabriel's hand slammed over mine, fixing the door in place. "Now that we're here, it'll be easier if we just move forward with the interview."

I snorted. "Easier for you, maybe." I tried to hold the door in place while sliding out from under his grasp, but his grip was firm. He put more pressure on

THE SECRET SHADOW

the door. The muscles in my arm began to tremble.

I glared at him. "Why don't you do your job and go find the real lawbreaker? I have better things to do, and you're wasting your time with me."

He surprised me by pulling back so fast that I almost fell through the open door after him. "I suppose we should interview someone else," he said to his fellow Guard.

Turning on his heel with a slightly vacant look, he left without another word.

The other guard frowned, glancing between us, then shrugged. She murmured to Gabriel as they moved away, "I *told* you about the special status…"

I stood there blinking a second or two longer before I shook myself out of the stupor and swung the door closed.

Leaning against it, I frowned. *That was odd.*

They'd moved on to the next room.

I peeked out, listening through a crack as they knocked.

The room beside mine had been vacant since I'd come to stay at the castle. Since this residence hall was set aside for council members, I knew the occupant, whoever they were, must be on one of the royal family councils.

No one responded. The second guard spoke,

"This occupant is listed as employed on another island for six months."

Gabriel grumbled, "We'll have to check the logs."

They moved on to the next hall, leaving mine empty.

All across the castle, other guards were conducting the same interviews. It was hard to guess how much time I had before they'd come back.

I let the door click softly closed.

Leaning back against the wood, I chewed on my nail, until it matched the others I'd gnawed on earlier.

While I might not be bothered again until morning, there was an equal chance that I might only have an hour or two before Gabriel returned.

It'd be foolish to question my good fortune when I should be taking advantage of it.

All that mattered right now was that they didn't come back until the other shifter had been caught—until *I* caught them.

Striding toward the wardrobe, I was already inside before it occurred to me: I still didn't have a real plan.

Guessing the shifter's location was really only the very beginning of a plan.

While it'd be easy enough to hide in the kitchen pantry until the shifter showed, the *capture* part still had me stumped.

It wouldn't do any good to find them if I lost them immediately.

I stepped out to pace the length of my room.

Every few rounds, I paused by the door to listen.

Glancing at the jar on my desk, my fingers trembled slightly. I didn't do well under stress.

This other shifter clearly knew how to use their abilities. They'd embraced their Gift, probably had years more experience than I did. Maybe they'd even had a mentor and real training.

A run in with someone like that could easily backfire, if I wasn't careful. It paled in comparison to being interviewed by the Guard though.

At least with the shifter, I had a chance.

If only because I had the element of surprise.

Earlier, I'd considered becoming a tiny poisonous phidar. I'd crawl up the oblivious shifters clothing until I found exposed skin, and sink my fangs in.

They'd never see it coming.

In that form, though, just one bite and the shifter wouldn't wake without the help of a castle healer. Possibly not even then.

Not to mention there was a very real possibility of being stepped on before I had a chance to bite anyone.

It was too risky.

Animal forms in general were limiting.

Maybe I could pretend to be a clueless servant—or even the king or queen? But if the shifter attacked me in those forms, I'd be more vulnerable...

I blew out the little candle by the bed and the room fell into darkness. I didn't need light to pace. At least I could pretend to be asleep while I schemed.

The hall was quiet. Only a hint of moonlight streamed in through my bedroom window.

Time was running out.

Desperation made me consider the Lucklore. A hulking beast with the head of an ox and the body of a bear, with bone-slicing claws the length of my fingers, dangerous horns, and sharp, wicked teeth.

But what would I do in that form? Cut the shifter into ribbons and deliver the pieces to the royal family?

There wasn't time for this debate. If I wasted any more time, the shifter might visit the kitchen and leave before I ever had a chance to confront them.

I needed to already be in place when the shifter

THE SECRET SHADOW
arrived.

If fortune worked in my favor, they'd be starving. Exhausted. Weak. Maybe they'd make a mistake.

Stepping back into the wardrobe, I pressed the dresses out of the way and closed the door behind me, traveling to the kitchen pantry before I could talk myself out of it.

I'd improvise if I had to.

If I couldn't think of a way to capture the other shifter, then at least I could get a glimpse of them and maybe follow them to wherever they were hiding.

Once in the kitchens, I immediately shifted into Farah, one of the serving girls who usually worked during the day. She shouldn't be anywhere near the kitchen at this time of night.

More importantly, if I accidentally stumbled into someone besides the shifter, no one would report seeing *my* face here.

With that larger shift complete, I followed it with a smaller shift of my inner-ear until it was shaped like an owls', making my hearing so acute that it could catch the smallest whisper of sound. I did this whenever I snuck into the kitchen, so I was used to it and only needed a minute to complete the change.

I crouched in the dark pantry, waiting.

The smaller shift gave me an idea.

I could transform a tiny part of myself into something poisonous and catch them unaware.

A small part of me whispered that learning minor shifts took a lot of practice. Time I didn't have right now.

Not helpful.

What mattered most wasn't using my Gift perfectly, but my ability to deceive. To make the shifter believe I was harmless and unimportant. Hadn't I been doing that my entire life?

I can do this.

Turning my teeth into the venomous fangs of the phidar wouldn't work. In a larger mouth, they were almost guaranteed to have too much venom.

I squeezed my eyes shut, trying to picture the book of creatures I'd studied in the library.

There was a cone snail. Tiny, but deadly, they had a single stinger. Shifting my finger into a stinger would probably end up fatal, since the true size of their stinger was closer to an eyelash.

I heard a rustling.

Leaning forward onto my knees, I peered out. If that was the shifter already, I needed an answer to

THE SECRET SHADOW

click into place in the next few seconds. My mind was blank.

When I cracked the pantry door open, it took a second for my eyes to adjust, but there was no one there.

After another pause, the rustling came again.

This time I could see what made the sound—it was just a towel fluttering in the breeze from an open window.

I sat back, blowing out a breath.

The hungry pit in my stomach ate away at me.

I scarfed down some old bread from one of the pantry shelves, trying to make it go away. But the ache didn't fade. It wasn't the hollow hunger that followed shifting. It was fear.

Stealth was my strong suit—if it came to a fight, I wasn't nearly as sure I could win, which meant poison was the answer. It was just a matter of finding a toxin that wouldn't kill the shifter instantly. I needed them alive if I was going to save my reputation and place in the castle.

Closing my eyes, I envisioned the book of creatures again. There was a blue-ringed octopi. My hopes rose. That was a better size. Then the text I'd read came back to me: the toxicity level could kill up to 26 Jinn.

What had been the creature on the next page…

My eyes flew open.

The poisonous dart frog.

Perfect.

It carried a similar paralyzing toxin that could be transmitted through the skin, but in a much smaller quantity. The recipient would never see it coming.

Best of all, I'd actually seen a dart frog once in the human rainforests with Shem. This firsthand knowledge should help me transform correctly.

Satisfied, I shifted the skin across the fingers of my right hand until they each turned vibrant blue with black spots, filled with the poisonous dart frog's toxins.

Then I pressed my sensitive ear to the pantry door to wait.

Ten minutes passed.

Then fifteen, twenty.

Thirty.

More.

My sense of time began to disintegrate.

It had to be nearing two in the morning.

My eyes burned, begging me to close them, but I forced my body to stay alert.

I wouldn't leave until I was one hundred percent

THE SECRET SHADOW

certain that the shifter wasn't coming.

But what if they already came and went?

Shoulders sagging, I scooted back until I sat on a sack of potatoes, dropping my head into my hands.

If I was forced to wait until tomorrow, it might be too late.

There was no guarantee the shifter would even return here.

This was a stupid plan.

Every second I spent not trying to escape, I might as well be locking myself in a cell in the dungeons below.

The Guard would come for me soon.

I'd fail the interview.

My leg tingled as my foot fell asleep beneath me. I wiggled around on the sack of potatoes, trying to find a more comfortable position. My right arm ached from the tension of holding my poisonous fingers away from the rest of my body. I rested it on a shelf. Without a mentor to teach me the inner workings of my Gift, I'd never learned if I could poison myself—and I wasn't going to risk finding out now.

Through the crack in the pantry door, the pitch black kitchens showed the first hints of dawn, only an hour or so away now. The kitchen staff would be here soon—including my look-alike, Farah. Shortly after that, the rest of the castle would rise, and I'd have wasted my entire night on this foolishness.

Exhaustion tugged at my eyelids. It'd make me even more likely to crack when interviewed by the Guard tomorrow.

I gritted my teeth, squeezing my burning eyes shut to stop the salty tears.

Time to give up.

I'd go back to my rooms and fight sleep as I tried to come up with a new plan.

Rubbing my backside as I stood, I stretched to ease the stiffness, then froze at a sound.

What was that?

I held my breath. It'd been the tiniest sigh of a door opening on the other side of the room.

Light footsteps sounded now on the stone floor.

They padded closer.

If it was a staff member, I'd be in trouble.

But what if it was the shifter?

It was too early to start breakfast—I gripped the door handle.

This was the chance I'd been hoping for.

I had to make it count.

With one last deep breath, I picked up a random

THE SECRET SHADOW

container, labeled "salt," taking care not to let my right hand touch any other part of my body.

I stepped out.

10

LETTING THE PANTRY DOOR close with a bang behind me, I was intentionally noisy, as if I hadn't been hiding there all along. This was part of the act, along with the apron I'd put on over my head when I'd first arrived.

Don't leave, I begged the shifter, even as I pretended not to notice their presence right away. Setting the container down on a random counter, keeping my shifted hand hidden behind it, I finally allowed my eyes to lift.

My heart sank.

It was just Naomi, one of the morning cooks.

I held back a groan.

Pretending to fold napkins, I snuck another glance at her from across the room.

She wasn't wearing her apron yet and her gray hair was uncovered, hanging down her back. Unusual to see when the cooks always kept their hair bound up during the day. But then, she was here before her shift started, likely too anxious over the latest castle drama to sleep. I couldn't blame her.

Now I'd have to pretend to be Farah, make some excuse to leave, and when the real Farah arrived, they'd realize it was another shifter sighting. That would add more fuel to the fire, and the Guard would work twice as fast to complete the interviews. It'd be all my fault when they got to me by midday.

Naomi moved slowly around the kitchen, ignoring me, opening cupboards in search of something.

I hesitated. Maybe I still had time to slip away.

Before I could decide, she turned in my direction, and her gaze briefly touched mine.

"Morning, Naomi," I said, when she didn't speak. My voice came out rough with its first use since the evening before and I cleared my throat.

"Morning," the older woman replied, but didn't

stop her search.

Something struck me as odd.

I couldn't quite put my finger on it.

Was it the way she scrounged through the cupboards as if she'd never seen the contents inside before?

Or maybe it was the sudden lack of concern for her long hair draping over kitchen counters where food was prepared—something Naomi would never have allowed if she'd seen anyone else do so…

As she continued to ignore my presence, my confidence grew. Naomi would've taken one glance at me, a lowly Jinni girl from the acropolis, and put me to work.

This wasn't Naomi.

It was the shifter.

"Can I help you find something?" I asked in a cheerful voice, with a respectful dip of my head. That's how servants always greeted me when I stopped by the kitchens.

I hadn't realized how stiff the shifter was until her posture relaxed. When she smiled back at me, I was struck with a strange sense of deja-vu. "I'm looking for some fruit."

"Here," I said as calmly as I could, while my

heart beat so hard it could knock my apron off. Careful to hide my hand covered in tree frog spots, I picked up the fruit bowl and carried it to her, clenching my toes in an effort to stay steady.

I held it out.

She slipped a bunch of bananas from the bowl, then pocketed an apple, and another, and a third.

I moved the bowl slightly to one side as she reached out again.

Our hands met.

I knew the poison was fast-acting, but I still gasped at the way her face paled.

She took a step back.

Then another.

Frowning, she stared down at her hand, then up at me, as her breathing grew ragged.

The toxin was taking effect.

"What kind of poison is this?" she murmured to herself.

She was so compelling, I almost answered.

Eyes closing, she sank to the floor, pulling in on herself and shutting me out.

I stood awkwardly over her, waiting.

Once she stopped moving, I'd run to fetch the Jinni Guard. Or maybe a healer first… She wasn't looking so good. Was she going to make it that long?

"Ah... yes," she whispered suddenly, between deep breaths.

Was it my imagination, or was her breathing returning to normal? It didn't make sense. That wasn't how the poison worked.

I gasped. *Her coloring!*

In the dim light of the kitchen, with her head buried in her knees and arms, I hadn't noticed—her skin was now a vibrant blue and black, just like my hand.

Like the poisonous dart frog.

If she'd shifted, did that mean she was immune to the poison?

I tensed, ready to travel instantly if need be.

But I held off, hoping I was wrong.

Maybe the poison was slower than I expected... I didn't want to lose this one chance if I could help it.

On a deep breath, she drew herself to her feet, back to me. Her gray hair shimmered, turning black, and her skin returned to normal.

What was she shifting into now?

A tremor ran through my body. Whatever her plan was, this couldn't be good.

Run! My instincts screamed, but I was too

frightened to react.

Especially when the shifter spoke in a calm voice, "Well done, darling, I'm impressed."

I went numb.

Impressed?

"Next time, consider a sleeping potion or enchantment instead." She turned to face me with a smile that was oddly affectionate. "Far more effective against another shape-shifter."

The words unstuck my feet.

I stumbled back, eyes glued to her face. It couldn't be…

She'd transformed into her true form: long, black hair, jade-green eyes, and a confidence in her stance that couldn't be feigned.

I knew it was her true form, because I knew *her*.

I took another step back.

She followed me, step for step.

My breath came in panicked gasps. I didn't have to pretend to be terrified.

"Sariah?" I said under my breath, too soft for her to hear. My back hit the counter where I'd gotten the fruit. Somewhere in the back of my mind, I registered the clatter of the bowl hitting the floor as I dropped it. The remaining apples and pears rolled around our feet. Neither of us glanced down.

She gave me the same steady, unyielding gaze as when I'd been a child.

The shifter is my mother.

11

I CAN STILL TURN *her in.*

That was my first thought. Followed immediately by, *Could I live with myself if I betrayed my mother?*

Standing there, breathing raggedly, I thought I knew the answer.

After the choices I'd made the last few months, if it was between me or her, I'd do whatever it took to survive. Especially since she'd done the same to me. She'd abandoned me to grow up alone with my father all those years ago.

But my feet didn't move. My arms dangled limp by my sides.

Giving myself a mental shake, I reached back and drew a butcher's knife from the wooden block on the counter. I held it out between us. "Don't move."

The corner of her mouth tilted up in a smile, but she didn't protest.

Time to call for a nearby guard.

I was going to turn in my own mother.

When I opened my mouth to yell... I couldn't do it.

I couldn't pretend she was a stranger and still turn her in.

Not when she was the only family I had left. Not when she'd finally come back, after all these years.

Her smile softened as she waited patiently.

I lowered the knife.

"Come now, Jezebel," she said. "Let's drop the pretense, shall we?"

My lips parted.

How does she knows it's me?

My poisonous fingers gave away my Gift, but how did she see through my disguise? Or... did she even know it was a disguise? It occurred to me that

THE SECRET SHADOW

she hadn't seen me grow up. That she didn't truly know what her own daughter looked like anymore.

Gripping the knife, a new fear flashed through my mind: what if my mother revealed my Gift to the Jinni Guard?

She knew it was me. And she'd seen me shift.

This was the woman who'd left me with my father without remorse, disappearing for years. I'd never gotten an apology or even an explanation. It wasn't hard to imagine her exposing my Gift, if it'd allow her to escape.

After wavering, I decided not to trust her further and remained in my false form. At least this way, if she betrayed me and named "Jezebel" as the shifter, she'd be pointing to a kitchen serving girl.

That would lessen her credibility.

It was best to assume this was her plan. If I expected the worst, I couldn't be surprised by it.

Still holding the knife, I made my voice cold, "What're you doing here?"

The early dawn light illuminated her face just enough that I caught a flash of something—disappointment? "I suppose that's fair. I shouldn't expect you to trust me after all these years. But I've seen your face, darling. After my attempt to get your information from the clerk failed, I braved the dining hall, and I would've recognized you anywhere. You don't need to wear this other girl's body for my sake."

I swallowed hard.

So much for my plans to confuse her.

She crossed her arms, waiting.

Fine.

Careful to check the windows and doors first, I shifted into my true form.

I forced my arms to stay loose at my sides, pulling my shoulders back and lifting my chin. "Do you truly recognize me?" I meant to sound sharp. Instead, I came across weak and unsure. I cringed inwardly.

"Of course," my mother widened her eyes. "I'd know your face anywhere." As I was about to soften, she ruined it by adding, "I also casually asked someone to point you out to be absolutely certain. I've been watching from a distance, waiting for the opportunity to talk to you."

"Why?" I stepped sideways as I spoke, subtly putting myself between her and the door. "Why have you been watching—more importantly, why are you here at all?"

"I came here looking for you," she replied,

answering without giving me any new information.

I frowned and repeated, "*Why?*"

Once again, she didn't answer directly, in typical Jinni fashion. "Rumors said you'd come to live here at the castle. I wanted to look at the books to confirm. How was I to know the servant I pretended to be was gone? It seemed like a simple way to gain access to the books—if they didn't lock them up, it would've been a lot easier." She laughed then, a soft, bell-like sound that teased my mind with buried memories.

"You've caused a lot of trouble for me, you know." I decided to be direct. There wasn't time to play games right now, with my fate in her fickle hands.

"How so?" she raised her brows innocently.

I didn't buy that for a second. "You revealed your Gift in front of the entire Jinni Guard—"

She scoffed lightly. "Not the *entire* Guard—"

"—and now they're looking for a shifter in the castle," I spoke over her. "You've jeopardized my position here."

"I swear to you, that wasn't my intention," she replied, but she didn't seem overly concerned.

It was my turn to scoff.

"Jezebel, I truly didn't mean to cause you pain." Her brows pinched together. I couldn't tell if it was annoyance or sincerity. "I should've researched more carefully before I infiltrated the castle staff."

"Too late now," I mumbled, feeling oddly childish.

All the things I'd wanted to say to her when I was a little girl came flooding into my mind.

Why did you leave? Why didn't you take me with you? Why did you never come back?

But none of them were worth saying out loud because I knew the answers already.

The answers had become clear years ago.

Because she didn't care.

My voice came out flat, "I'll ask one last time: why are you here?"

Spreading her hands wide, gesturing to the room where we stood, she tsked at me as if it were obvious. "For your 18th birthday, of course."

A small pang in my chest tried to make its way to my face.

I refused to show it.

With a sigh, as if bored, I shook my head. "My birthday was weeks ago."

She tilted her head and then sighed as well, glancing around the room and twisting her hands instead of meeting my eyes. "All right. It was more than that."

Was she finally going to be honest with me? I tried not to hold my breath.

"I have someone back home who watched over you from a distance. To be my eyes and ears while I was away. They checked in on you now and then to make sure you were well. They kept me updated."

I blinked a few times, letting this revelation sink in. Did that mean she *did* care? But if so, why couldn't she have sent this person to take me in when my father became unbearable? Or bring me to her? It didn't make sense.

When I didn't respond, she continued, "They sent word that the old apartment was occupied by a new family. And that you and your father were nowhere to be seen. I had to come back, to make sure you were well."

Once again, I shook my head. Unable to help myself, I crossed my arms and tried to subtly put pressure on my chest to stop the pain there. "I've been in the castle for weeks now—over two months."

I didn't address the part about my father, banking on the fact that she'd never cared about him before, and she likely wouldn't start now.

Her gaze took in my closed-off expression, crossed arms, and stiff back, before drifting to the floor, as if the answer lay somewhere at my feet. "Coming back was an enormous risk," she said more softly, sounding unsure of herself for the first time. "I had to put plans into place, prepare multiple escape routes…" she trailed off.

That triggered a memory. A vision of her in armor—real armor, not the decorative kind that so many Jinn wore as a fashion statement. Not just a simple breastplate or arm plates, but full head to toe armor. If I closed my eyes, I could see the spot on the table where she used to set her helmet at the end of the day.

"You used to be in the Guard," I whispered, remembering again what the queen had said about an "unfortunate encounter" with a shifter. I narrowed my eyes to study her more closely.

She dipped her head in acknowledgment.

What did she do to make them so terrified?

Maybe one of my questions was still worth asking. I tried to sound nonchalant, but my voice came out soft, almost shaking. "Why did you leave me?"

As soon as the words left my lips, I wished I could take them back. I didn't know if I wanted the answer. She'd left because she didn't love me enough to stay. It was that simple. Hearing her say it out loud would only make the pain fresh.

I drew a breath to say never mind, but she spoke first, "It's a long story. Let's just say the Jinni Guard might know exactly which shifter they're looking for."

When she said that, she didn't look scared in the slightest.

The knife slipped through my fingers. It clattered onto the stone floor. "You were expecting to be discovered."

"Not that quickly," she replied in a wry tone. "I should've researched more carefully before choosing that particular Jinni form. Faulty information, but I still could've checked my sources."

If she'd anticipated being exposed, then she also had to know how the Jinni Guard would react. What she'd said earlier finally registered: *multiple escape routes.*

She had an exit strategy.

A muscle twitched in my jaw. She was going to leave me behind once more, after sentencing me to the worst fate in all of Jinn.

If she could betray me a second time, then I could do the same.

I allowed my irritation to show and turned away,

using it as an excuse to scan the kitchen. Most of the counters were wiped clean and bare, but there were a few cast iron pans on a drying rack.

"Your birthday gift to me was to cause the entire Jinni Guard to search for a shifter?" I swallowed, throat tight. I tried to match her casual tone, not completely succeeding. "I wish you hadn't left behind a trail that leads directly to me."

"I didn't intend to do that," she protested.

When I refused to look at her, she reached out, clutching my arm. "Jezebel, I swear to you, I didn't know." She sighed. "I should've guessed. But before tonight, I had no idea I'd passed on this Gift."

I finally met her gaze, searching.

Her eyes were shadowed in the dark, seeming dark grey instead of the green I knew they were, but there was enough early dawn light to see her tentative smile.

She let go of my arm, but didn't step back. "I won't waste your time. Especially when we both know this isn't the safest place for us right now." Clearing her throat, she clasped her hands in front of her, and this time her voice cracked. "I came to ask if you'd leave with me."

"Leave?" I squeaked, taken aback. I coughed,

and tried again, but it still came out higher-pitched than I meant it to, "With you?"

"Yes. I'd like you to come with me to the human world. I've made a home there, and I believe you'd be happy," she continued. "I realize I haven't been here for you the past few years."

"Twelve," I corrected in a flat tone. "Twelve years."

She shrugged, as if that didn't matter. "You had your father. I was on the run in the human world. I promise I'll explain everything when we have the time, but it was for the best. Trust me."

I scoffed. Moving toward the pan, I crossed my arms and allowed myself to sulk visibly. Let her think that was why I was moving away. Hopefully, she would follow and fall right into my trap.

She did.

As I turned, I found her much closer than I'd anticipated. With the drying rack directly behind me, I let my hand drift back to wrap around the handle of the pan. It'd only take one step plus a solid swing. She'd be out cold.

I'd call for the Guard and explain that I'd caught her shifting. They'd take her away. It'd be over, just like that.

Swallowing again, I sucked in a deep breath

around the tight muscles in my throat.

"I *am* sorry," my mother whispered, when I didn't say anything else.

I waited, expecting more.

Nothing.

My hand gripped the pan.

I tensed, preparing to swing. *It's nothing she wouldn't do to you.* My muscles trembled, but my body wouldn't move.

I couldn't do it.

As much as I wanted to, I couldn't hurt my own mother, even if she'd hurt me like this before. Even if she *was* the shifter they were looking for. Even if she deserved it.

My eyes watered.

When my mother brushed away the first tear that trickled down my cheek, they only fell harder. She reached behind me to take my hand and slowly pried my fingers off the pan, one by one. Then, gently, she pulled me into her arms and hugged me.

Despite myself, I sank into the warmth that I'd missed so much all these years.

I sobbed.

"Shhh." She rubbed my back, setting the pan down with a soft thunk on the counter. "I know. I've been in your shoes. If I'd known you'd developed this Gift, I'd have found a way to come back sooner and help you." She pulled back a bit so she could see my face, tipping my chin up and frowning at me. "My source never saw a single sign." She studied me closer. "You hid it so well, I'd never have guessed if I hadn't seen it myself?"

She phrased it like a question, like she wanted to know why I hadn't revealed it to anyone.

I shook her arms off and stepped back. "Tell me," I said, unable to hold back some of the bitterness. "Did it go well for you when you revealed your own Gift?" Knowing the answer, having grown up with her complaints about my father and everyone else using her, I spoke before she could, "No. So why would I expose myself?"

"Fair point." She surprised me by smiling again. "You remind me so much of myself at your age."

I wrapped my arms tighter around myself. If the counter hadn't been directly behind me, I'd have taken a step back. "You might want a reunion right now, but I don't have the time. I'm too busy trying to avoid being framed for what *you* did." I ripped my gaze away and glared out the window, not wanting her to see more tears.

Her presence hadn't really changed anything.

The Jinni Guard still had to catch a shifter.

It was either her or me.

If anything, I had more problems now because I didn't trust her. She might give them *my* name. That meant it was in my best interest not to turn her in—at least until I knew if she'd keep my secrets. Which meant I was back to square one: no way to escape and about to be caught.

"What if you didn't have to worry about the Guard anymore?" my mother interrupted my dismal thoughts.

Glancing over my shoulder, I frowned. "I don't see a way around them…"

"Like I said," she spoke slowly. "I came to ask if you'd like to leave with me. You're not safe here. It was only a matter of time before something gave you away—if they weren't looking for you now, they'd be looking for you next month or next year, because at some point, you'll leave a trail. Trust me."

There were those two words again. *Trust me.*

I didn't.

But I *did* want answers.

The kitchen walls were turning golden with the first hints of sunrise. Someone could enter at any moment.

"Why should I?" I demanded. "You broke my trust when you left. You can't honestly believe I'd go with you, even if we could lift the enchantment spell locking us inside the castle."

"Don't worry about that, darling." My mother waved away my worries. "It's nothing I can't handle. If you come with me, I'll teach you multiple ways to get around enchantments, as well as dozens of other things a mentor should've shown you."

It was as if she knew my weakness.

When I'd first discovered my Gift, I'd wanted a mentor more than anything. Everyone else's Gifts had flourished under careful supervision and training, while mine grew stagnant. I'd been isolated. I still wondered sometimes what might've happened if I'd had more guidance—if Asher would've been able to force my hand and if my friends would still be gone.

A mentor would change everything for me.

While I didn't want to leave Shem behind, I was surprisingly tempted.

As I wavered, she cocked her head to the side, turning as if something had caught her attention.

The heavy kitchen door groaned.

Around the corner, still out of sight, someone shuffled into the kitchen.

We both froze.

A loud thunk sounded as they put a wooden door block in place, and then their footsteps whispered across the floor, heading in our direction.

My mother reacted first, leaning forward to whisper in my ear, "I understand this is all a bit sudden. Sleep on it. I'll find you later."

Before I could reply, she vanished.

A split second passed before I shook myself out of my stupor and traveled too, flashing back into the wardrobe in my room.

Four dark wooden walls surrounded me with the dresses still pressed against one side. The fabric rustled as I sank into a crouch. *What just happened?*

With my hands over my face, I drew a few deep breaths, struggling to find a sense of control after my entire foundation had been shaken.

Stepping out of the wardrobe, I fell face first onto the bed, exhausted. My body sank gratefully into the soft mattress.

I should try to think of a new plan, but all I could think of was catching a few hours of sleep before facing my imminent doom.

12

A FIST BANGING ON my door woke me. Sun streamed in with full force, making it clear I'd slept away most of the morning.

Is it already time for the noon meal? I blinked away the fuzzy remnants of sleep, dragging myself out of bed. Yesterday's dress was wrinkled from sleeping in it. As I turned to the door I paused. *I never called for anyone to bring a meal...*

It was the Guard, coming for my interview. It had to be.

A reply caught in my throat. If I wasn't here,

they couldn't accuse me of missing an interview…

Without giving myself a chance to second guess, I rushed to the wardrobe and stepped inside. I shut the door softly, then traveled.

They couldn't interview me if they couldn't find me.

Reappearing one hall over from the council chambers, I sagged against the wall, breathing hard, as if I'd run around the entire castle instead of across my little room.

Close call.

I was safe for now.

Unfortunately, unless I found a more permanent way out of the interviews, it wouldn't last.

I threw my shoulders back and forced myself to breathe deeply as the rising panic threatened to take over.

Long moments passed.

It was only noon.

I didn't have a plan or even the first hint of one, but I couldn't stand here all day.

Glancing down, I groaned.

I was still wearing yesterday's dress.

The council already judged my every move. If I was seen in the same outfit two days in a row, they'd

THE SECRET SHADOW

not only mock me for my attire, they'd start asking more dangerous questions. Either way, it wasn't worth drawing their attention.

Glancing around, I slipped into one of the little alcoves that lined the hallways, holding décor. I'd hoped to hide my shifting behind one of many full-blown suits of armor, often displayed from historical Jinni battles, or at the very least behind a vase filled with ever-blooming flowers. This one held only a painting featuring an ancient royal I didn't recognize. It'd have to do.

Pressing back against the wall, after checking the empty hall once more to make sure I wouldn't have an audience, I shifted my gown.

I couldn't do much beyond simple color changes and shape, but I tried to make it count. The forest green color turned a dark red. Where the fabric split to tastefully reveal one leg, I couldn't force it together, but I was able to lengthen the straps of my sandals where they circled my calves. I then turned them from tan to black, until they swirled delicately around my thigh, becoming a pattern of sorts before disappearing beneath the red fabric. The only other change I could think of was to raise the sweetheart neckline until it stretched to my neck, wrapping it around and leaving my back bare.

No one would believe it was the same dress.

Satisfied, I stepped out of the alcove. In the past I'd been tempted to create more striking shifts—I could've easily formed butterfly wings or peacock feathers that would've shocked the court with their realism—because they would've *been real*—but ultimately, I'd decided it wasn't worth the risk. If someone ever tried to search my wardrobe, I couldn't explain the absence of such a memorable gown.

Striding around the corner toward the council door, the guard there was unusually quick to grant me admission. I barely noticed, too desperate to find Shem and ask him to extend my immunity. He was my only hope.

When I entered, I jerked to a halt.

The entire council was gathered.

Colorful gazes around the room all turned to me, pinning me in place. I'd never seen this room so full. Almost three dozen council members filled the chairs, spilling past them to stand around the edges of the room and the balcony above. Shem must've called an emergency meeting and every single council member was in attendance.

Except me.

Shem paused in speaking to turn, and relief

THE SECRET SHADOW

flooded his features as he let out a breath. "Jezebel. Thank goodness, you're all right. I was told no one could find you, but you must've got my message."

The knock on the door. Embarrassed, I managed to nod and duck my head, murmuring apologies as I pushed through the crowd without looking at anyone. *It hadn't been the Guard, it'd been Shem's messenger.* I found an open space to stand along one side.

As the heat of humiliation faded, though, I scowled at the Jinn around me. Whoever'd told him they couldn't find me hadn't even tried; before his messenger, no one else had knocked on my door.

"As I was saying," Shem resumed his speech, meeting the eyes of Jinn around the room as he spoke. "The Guard will continue to do interviews throughout the day. They should be able to complete them by this evening at the latest. We can expect them to begin working with council members near the end of the day."

No.

I shivered. I had roughly half a day left of freedom.

The thunder of my pulse in my ears made it hard to hear what Shem said next. I took slow breaths, focusing on drawing the air in and then out at the same pace. To say I was running out of time would be like saying the room was crowded—so obvious that it was suffocating.

"I called this meeting to ask that we conduct the council interviews here, in the back rooms," Shem was saying as I forced myself to pay attention. "To help it go as quickly and smoothly as possible."

I hadn't thought it possible to tense further, but the muscles in my back and shoulders spasmed painfully.

There'd be no escape here in the council chambers. No wardrobe to run to.

No privacy either.

I could envision the whole spectacle as if it were happening now—everyone would watch as I stepped into the back room with a guard. Jaws would drop as they dragged me back out again a few short minutes later. They'd declare that I was the hidden shifter and haul me to the dungeons to await my fate.

"Your highness," someone spoke up.

Chairs creaked around the room as dozens of Jinn shifted in their seats to look at the speaker. It was an elderly Jinni with streaks of silver in his hair and thinly veiled irritation. "May I ask what these interviews will consist of?"

"Of course." Shem moved to lean against a tall table, as if he needed the support. He stared at his hands for a moment. Inhaling, he straightened to look at all of us. "They're using a spell that pulls the truth from you. I allowed them to test it on me—" his mouth twisted upward slightly on one side. "With restrictions. Just a few pre-determined questions." He fiddled with the rings on his fingers, eyes falling to them, then stilled. "I tried to resist." Glancing up, his eyes met mine briefly. He smiled and said in a lighter tone, "I was curious."

A chuckle spread across the room.

I couldn't help but smile back, picturing it.

It was so like him. Always curious.

"It was…" his voice grew so soft that those in the back leaned forward. "I would call it uncomfortable. Heavy… I couldn't resist for more than a few seconds."

Swallowing hard, I tried to hide my anxiety, but it wasn't necessary. Nervous murmurs filled the air.

"None of you have anything to worry about," Shem spoke over the rising volume in a reassuring tone. "You merely need to speak the truth."

This was worse than I'd thought.

As I listened to Shem share more about the enchantment, I stiffened my resolve: I had to avoid this interview at all costs.

My mind ran through my limited choices for the thousandth time. There were really only two: besides getting caught—which was *not* an option—I could either flee or lead the Guard to another shifter.

My mother had offered a chance to escape with her, whatever that meant.

I might have to take her up on it.

As far as I knew, there weren't any other shifters in the castle. Even if I was wrong, they'd never reveal themselves now. With a day and a half or less, finding another shifter to turn in besides my mother was impossible.

I paused, chewing on the inside of my lip.

An idea slowly formed.

While my mother and I might be the only true shifters in the castle, the Guard didn't know that.

It was far-fetched, dangerous, and maybe not even possible, but it might work.

I can frame someone.

13

***"IF YOU'D LIKE TO** volunteer,"* Shem was saying, and my attention snapped back to him. *Volunteer for the interview?* I barely caught myself from scoffing out loud. *Never.* "You can approach any member of the Guard, and they'll direct you."

This caused a stir across the room. Or rather the absence of one, as every Jinni in the room grew still and an unnatural quiet settled over us.

Obviously volunteering would look good to the royal family. But it wouldn't happen. Every single person here had secrets. It didn't matter if they were related to shape-shifting or not—a truth spell was incredibly vulnerable. No one wanted to submit to the Guard.

Shem deflated slightly at the reaction. "If you'd rather wait for your turn, I completely understand. However, I must ask that you please do not roam the halls in the meantime, as it will make the guards work more difficult. If you're comfortable waiting here until the end of the day, we'll have food brought up for meals. But if you'd rather return to your rooms, just let the guard at the door know where we can find you before you leave."

With that, he ended the meeting abruptly.

Conversation slowly picked up in murmurs. A few council members approached Shem.

I stayed where I was.

There might still be time to frame someone, if I worked fast. Hopefully I had at least a few more hours. I needed to test every angle, make sure nothing would go wrong, and find an unsuspecting Jinni.

Though some council members remained seated, the chairs around me emptied rapidly. I slipped into a small blue velvet chair in the corner until the noon meal was delivered.

While some tried to discuss unrelated things, the main subject as everyone gathered to eat was the interviews. I tried to tune it out, keeping to myself.

On my right, a quiet woman named Eden leaned forward, hands pressed over her brow. Whenever I saw her, she was alone. If I framed her, would anyone speak up?

As if in answer, another council member approached the table, taking the seat beside her and rubbing her back. He murmured that they'd catch this awful shape-shifter soon.

I sighed, turning away from the sight.

I'd forgotten about her husband. He'd likely fight the accusation, making it harder to stick.

Finishing my meal, I couldn't listen to them calmly discuss the interviews any longer. I left the table to casually walk around the room, searching for the right person to frame.

My gaze landed on a Jinni by the bookshelves named Noam. He hadn't moved since the meeting, besides an urgent tapping of his foot.

I imagined shifting into his form. I could stroll out in front of a Guard member—Gabriel maybe—and then shift again. I could choose an animal that was difficult to catch—something with wings perhaps. Once out of sight, I'd return to my own form and then hide in my room while they hunted.

Noam wouldn't see them coming. They'd find him immediately and interrogations would begin. Would they question him much, if they'd seen him shift with their own eyes? If he had an alibi or could prove his innocence, it might only be a temporary solution.

But perhaps, considering the way he was tapping that foot, he had his own secrets that could distract the Guard for a while.

I sucked in a breath, trying to ignore the twinge of guilt at framing someone I barely knew who hadn't done anything to me.

It felt like what I'd done to Asher all over again. In some ways, at the core, it was exactly the same, because it boiled down to one thing: survival. It was either him or me.

As always, if I had to save myself, I'd do it. *Whatever it takes.*

Turning to the window, I pretended to stare out at the stunning landscape, stretching out in the distance, so no one would notice what I was really looking at: Noam's reflection where he sat behind me.

There was still one enormous flaw in my plan

though. Both Noam and I had to leave this room for it to work. In his case, he needed to leave because staying here would give him an obvious alibi. Meanwhile, I had to somehow get out of this room without anyone noticing that I'd ever left to keep my own alibi intact.

I stayed there for a long time, keeping Noam in the corner of my eye. But he didn't leave, or even move, except to make up a plate of leftover food from the noon meal and return to his seat.

I couldn't slip away either without drawing suspicion. Not when the only way out was past the Guard. They'd make careful note that I'd left.

All around the room, tension built as the hours passed.

Dinner arrived. It was a light fare, since not many felt like eating.

I was running out of time.

"Ah, Jezebel," Jerusha's voice snaked up my spine, making me tense. "So good of you to join us earlier."

Turning to face her, I found Milcah, Dorcas, and a few other council members I'd worked with on occasion, Salman and Kareem, in her wake. I'd never worked closely with them. But I knew from experience that Kareem was a flirt, while Salman went out of his way to avoid me because, in Milcah's words, "He prefers not to speak to new council members until they've gotten a few years—or decades—of experience."

They stopped in front of me now, like a pack of wolves circling their prey.

Jerusha absently pet the thick white fur collar along the neck of her dress, which only added to my mental image. "Yes, I'm sure Prince Shem appreciated you attending the mandatory meeting."

My face flushed.

I tried to remember Shem's training back when I'd first arrived here. *Don't give them any ground. Don't reveal the effect of their words. That will only turn them into sharks with blood in the water.*

My cheeks burned under their intimidating gazes.

Too late.

I should frame one of them, not poor Noam. Unlike him, if Jerusha or Milcah had to undergo an interrogation from the guard, I wouldn't feel guilty at all.

Straightening my spine, I pretended a cheerfulness I didn't feel. "Yes, I understand someone sent for me? I'm sure I'll receive that

THE SECRET SHADOW

message about this meeting eventually."

I doubted they'd ever sent one. If not for Shem's messenger, I wouldn't have known of it at all.

It wasn't my best comeback, but I was frazzled at the moment.

Always, if possible, turn their words back on them, Shem's voice came to me. As usual, I struggled to do so. *They* hadn't been late to the meeting.

Milcah's eyes narrowed slightly, calculating. "Were you not in your rooms for the messenger to reach you?" The question seemed innocent, but they were leading me somewhere... What if they actually *had* sent someone?

"I was sleeping," I replied lamely. "They should have knocked louder." I needed to get out of this conversation as soon as possible.

Turn their words back on them.

If they were insinuating that I might be the shifter, I could do the same. "If the shifter was pretending to be a council member, they'd be the *first* to arrive at a meeting, to avoid suspicion." I paused for a second before I drew my brows together. "What time did you say you got here?"

Milcah's answering chuckle was forced. "Fair point, dear."

I *hated* being called that.

Framing either her or Jerusha would be almost gratifying. I crossed my arms, considering. While Jerusha liked to condescend, Milcah had gone out of her way to actually damage my relationship with Shem.

I made my decision.

Smiling at her, I didn't bother to reply.

There was something about holding a secret power over her, knowing what I was about to do, that took away her edge and made her seem small.

As if she could feel the change, she frowned. Gesturing to the others, she said, "This whole unpleasantness is exhausting. I'm going to go lie down in my room for an hour or two. I'm sure it's not my turn for a little while yet anyway."

She headed toward the door, while the others broke off to join nearby groups.

My hopes rose. Milcah had just solved half of my problems for me without even realizing it. Alone in her rooms, she'd be easy to frame.

All that was left now was finding a way to sneak out of here unnoticed.

I blew out a breath.

With only one exit, barred by the Guard, that would be a challenge.

"Were they bothering you?" Shem's voice behind me made me jump.

When I turned to face him, my smile was genuine. "Nothing I can't handle, thanks to your tutoring," I teased, keeping my tone lighthearted to hide how unsettled I was.

His shook his head as if he didn't believe it for a second. "You don't deserve this constant ribbing. I'm growing tired of the culture in the castle that shuns outsiders instead of welcoming. We should be more open to change."

The fact that he'd noticed should've lifted the weight, but I was starting to wonder if I'd ever find my footing here.

He rubbed the back of his neck unconsciously, as he gazed around the room, both of us aware of multiple council members subtly watching our exchange. "I wish we could escape this madness together," he said with a sigh. "I don't think I realized how much I'd missed our adventures."

I didn't know what to say. "Me too," I whispered.

He was the calm in the storm swirling around me. For one brief moment, I could take a full breath.

"How are you handling the stress of the last few days?" he asked and the next wave of anxiety came crashing down.

The Guard was coming, I was a threat, and my solution was still full of holes.

"It's been... challenging," I said, choosing a word that didn't really reveal anything. "But I wouldn't want you to worry over me. You have enough going on."

He let out a soft laugh. "Enough going on could qualify as a grave understatement. But that doesn't mean I don't have time to care."

About me.

It was unspoken, but the implication hovered over us.

"Thank you," I murmured, leaning forward. "I've been concerned about you as well."

Not for the reasons he might think, of course, since I knew he was in no danger from a shape-shifter.

"Well, no need to fear much longer," he replied, relaxing back on his heels, putting his hands in his pockets. "It's only a matter of hours before the shifter is caught and brought to justice. I have complete faith in the Guard."

I dropped his gaze immediately, unable to hide the sheer panic that caused. I hoped he would

THE SECRET SHADOW

misread my reaction as shyness.

His feet moved into view, and his warm hand came up to cover mine, as he tilted my chin up with the other. Waiting until I met his gaze, he repeated, "On my life, Jezebel, you're safe here."

Tears formed against my will.

Blinking quickly, I tried to hold them back. One slipped through. He caught it on my cheek, wiping it gently away.

"Thank you," I whispered finally, because I had to say *something*. He had no idea how false that was, but that wasn't his fault.

I swallowed the rest of the tears building in my throat, trying to find a peace I didn't feel.

Turning my fingers over in his hand where he still held mine, I touched his skin lightly. "It means a great deal to me to hear you say that."

He gently squeezed my hand in response, not letting go. "You look like you need to get away from this chaos for a little bit."

I held on like he was an anchor in the midst of a storm, attempting a small smile. "You see right through me. But I don't want to unnecessarily draw anyone's suspicions in a time like this…" I waved in the direction Jerusha and Milcah had gone, knowing he'd understand exactly what I meant.

He gave a short laugh, shaking his head. "Understandably so."

Gazing at him, I felt safe. Enough so to softly add, "I just wish I could go back to my room and lie down for a bit…"

His eyes grew a little vacant, and I thought he was about to pull away, when he surprised me by nodding. "I might have a solution."

I stilled.

With a hand on my arm, Shem turned us slightly so his back was to the room and lowered his voice. "Use the staircase. Make it seem like you're going up to the balcony or the library to read a book. No one will think twice about it."

I squinted, trying to understand what he was saying.

Even softer, he added, "As long as both doors are shut, and no one sees, you can travel."

I stared at the unassuming door to the stairs, eyes widening.

He nodded. "The staircase is my version of your wardrobe."

I quickly slammed my jaw shut, hiding my surprise from anyone watching by pretending to fix my hair. I'd never have guessed that.

"You're revealing your private traveling room?" I whispered. "To me?"

As far as I was aware, no other council member knew of this. Jinn protected their privacy, and the royal family even more so.

"I'm happy to," he replied, though his eyes still seemed slightly empty. He blinked and the feeling was gone. Maybe I'd imagined it. "Especially if it keeps you from traveling the halls. I worry for your safety when you're alone."

I waved a hand. "I promise I'll be fine."

"It's not just the shifter." Clearly he'd noticed my skepticism this time. I needed to hide it better. "The Guard has also been marking those who've undergone the interview so that they can see at a glance who's been through it."

Marking.

"How?" I whispered. The back of my neck tingled in premonition. "What does it look like?" Something told me this was another step on my path toward the dungeons.

"I don't know. Only my father and the Guard know. But apparently I have it."

I pulled back to look at him more closely. His pale eyes lacked their usual energy and his dark hair hung even more disheveled than normal, but otherwise he seemed the same. "I don't see anything."

"Exactly." He raised a brow. "So you have nothing to fear. The shifter has no idea how close we are to catching them."

A shiver raced through me. I had to clench my jaw to avoid my teeth chattering. *Oh, I have some idea.*

"Now go," he said with a smile, seeming a little more like his old cheerful self. "I'll make sure the Guard and this nosy council of mine never know you left."

Swallowing hard, I stepped closer to Shem and placed a hand on his arm, raising on my tiptoes to kiss his cheek, which was more than I'd ever dared to do. "Thank you," I whispered, meaning it more than he knew.

Now I had both an alibi *and* an escape from this room all in one.

Shem had just given me the opportunity to frame Milcah.

14

HEART POUNDING AS I left the prince behind, I moved toward the staircase.

Conversation buzzed around me as I wove through the main floor, overhearing gossip about who the shifter might be. I didn't stop to talk or meet anyone's gaze.

Most council members remained on the main floor, but I still had to take the stairs up and then back down twice before the staircase was finally empty.

I waited for the doors at both ends to shut.

Immediately, I traveled.

Landing in my room, I entered through the wardrobe as usual, breathing an enormous sigh of relief.

But even here, the pressure on my chest didn't let up.

My comfortable room was beginning to feel like a prison cell.

Maybe my mother had the right idea. As each passing hour dragged on, I grew more tempted to leave with her.

If my plan didn't work perfectly, I might still have to.

This constant dread was giving me a headache.

I pressed my hands to my temples, rubbing circles in an attempt to ease the steady throbbing.

Ever since my mother had arrived, a hopelessness had slowly started to swallow me up. I couldn't breathe. I couldn't think. I couldn't seem to catch a break.

But if the Guard began interviewing the council soon, they might clear Milcah of suspicion before I had the chance to frame her.

Adrenaline surged.

I was out of time.

Stepping up to the full-length mirror that hung

on my wall, I ran through the hazy plan one last time to solidify the details.

Milcah should be alone in her room by now. For the next hour or so, she shouldn't have an alibi.

On the other hand, as far as the Guard was aware, I was still in the council chambers. Since Shem had declared everyone must ask permission to leave, my own defense would be ironclad.

Once I shifted into Milcah's form, I simply needed to walk out my door and find the nearest guard.

Then, as Milcah, I'd shift again, right in front of their eyes—maybe into a Lacklore though, instead of a bird? That way, if the guard tried to use their crystal spear, I could knock them down with a massive paw...

I nodded to myself, and my reflection nodded back.

While the guard was unconscious or on the run from the dreaded shifter, I'd find a hidden alcove to return to my own form, travel to the council room through Shem's secret loophole in the staircase, and simply wait for the official announcement that the shifter was caught.

Milcah could be named the shifter within the hour.

The plan will work, I tried to reassure myself.

Using the mirror, I stepped close enough to see every detail and began to shift.

Eyes first. Then face, hair, body, and finally, an attempt at her swooping forest-inspired dress that she'd worn to the meeting earlier. I couldn't quite get the greenery right—it'd looked like actual branches encircling her long legs, with revealing but subtle glimpses of skin. Hopefully, no one would think to question any minor differences.

At the bottom mirror, movement caught my eye.

A thin strip of wood peeled away from the rest.

I stopped breathing.

Between one blink and the next, a tiny insect-like creature became a slender Jinni woman, forcing me to back up or be squished.

My mother.

How long had she been here?

She moved to sit on my desk, studying my new form, frowning. "Is this a spontaneous shift or are you planning something?"

I blinked, trying to orient myself. No "hello" or "how are you handling the pressure?" I pressed my lips together, unsure I wanted to share my plans. Instead, I gestured toward her. "What kind of creature was that?"

"The humans call it a 'Walking Stick'," she said with a grin, hopping off the desk and moving toward the window, glancing outside before continuing to wander the room. "They're not the most creative."

"Who? The Walking Stick?" I frowned.

She laughed as she traced the carvings on my bed post, swinging around one before peering into the attached bathing room. "No, the humans. The Walking Stick itself is actually quite creative when it comes to hiding in plain sight."

"Is that something you do often?" I asked boldly. Why bother beating around the bush, when she clearly didn't?

"All the time," she replied, grinning as she faced me finally. "Now, tell me." She waved at my disguise. "What is all this about?"

I hesitated. Might as well tell her. "Milcah is going to be our shifter. You and I will be safe once they think it's her."

For some reason, I expected a bit of approval or at least a hint that she was impressed.

Instead, she twisted her lips to one side, head tilting, then shook her head. "This plan seems underdeveloped."

I scoffed. "How much *development* does it really

need? Pretending to be someone else is fairly straightforward for the two of us."

She ignored my sarcasm. "The Guard is alert and quick on their feet. And they have Gifts you don't even know exist. What if they're able to capture you? It wouldn't matter if they knew who you were or not—you'd still end up in the dungeons."

Rubbing my eyes, I sighed. "Then I'll wait to shift into an animal form until I'm out of reach." When she opened her mouth to argue again, I added, "And I'll shift multiple times. By the time they think to look for a different animal or person, I'll be long gone."

One brow rose skeptically. "It's still reckless. All it would take is one deviation from the plan—one little detail going wrong—and the trail would lead directly back to you."

I crossed my arms, and a long pause stretched between us.

She's right.

I blew out a breath. "It's the only plan I have!" I never yelled like that. Stepping back, I dropped onto my bed, lowering my head into my hands. It was too much. She'd just torn my last remaining hope into shreds.

THE SECRET SHADOW

"You also have to consider, how long would this solution even last?" My mother continued mercilessly. "Once they find out whoever *this* is—" she waved a hand at Milcah's body—"she'll most likely find a way to prove her innocence in a few short weeks or even days. Then what? If they ask who framed her, who will she consider first?"

I swallowed hard.

Even if she *didn't* suspect me, my name would likely still be the first one on Milcah's lips.

"And what if they don't lower the enchantments around the castle while they interrogate her? You wouldn't even get the opportunity to run. And you would *have* to run eventually, because this is only a temporary solution."

I clenched my jaw and looked away. I wanted her to be wrong. Desperately.

But the truth was, she had a point.

If Milcah showed her face as I tried to frame her, it'd be over. If they *caught* me while framing her, it was over. If anyone suspected there was more going on than met the eye? Over.

"I told you I had a way to leave, darling," my mother said when I didn't answer. "You don't need to put yourself through all this emotional distress."

I flushed. "I don't *want* to leave." As soon as the

words left my mouth, I blinked in surprise. I couldn't remember the last time I'd been so candid with anyone. Not even myself. But at this point, I didn't have anything left to lose. In a whisper, I added, "I don't have a choice anymore."

My mother tilted her head, studying me. "You always have a choice," she said with a slight frown. "You're one of the most powerful Jinn in the world. You simply need to decide what you want and then make it happen."

"I want to *stay*." I said immediately.

She shrugged. "So stay."

A knock sounded on the door before I could answer.

I leapt off the bed, panicking at the sight of the hands fluttering up to my mouth.

They weren't *my* hands.

I was still in Milcah's form.

Could I frame her now? Coming out of *my* room? Not likely.

Quickly, I shifted back to my own form.

It wasted precious seconds.

As I did, I wondered darkly if maybe I should just give myself up.

At this point, probably nothing could save me.

THE SECRET SHADOW

"I didn't think the Guard would come back again so soon," I whispered in despair, unable to make my feet move toward the door.

My mother laughed lightly and waved me forward. "It's not the Guard."

I still didn't move. "How could you possibly know that?"

She grinned as she moved toward the wardrobe to hide in the corner, out of sight. "Because I ordered a noon meal delivered."

My jaw dropped. "You let them *see you*?"

Again, she chuckled, shaking her head. "Of course not. I let them see *you*."

Lips parting, I stared at her. She could successfully impersonate me after only our brief meeting in the kitchen earlier? It took me ages to convincingly shift into another Jinni—even Milcah's form was difficult for me, despite enduring her company for months now. Was this something I could learn under her tutelage? A longing stole over me as I was torn between wanting to stay and wishing I could take her up on her offer to leave this place and mentor me.

My mother made a shooing motion with her hands, distracting me from the internal debate. "Hurry up. I'm starving."

Swallowing hard, I forced myself to open the door. Sure enough, it was someone from the kitchen. Instead of letting the serving girl carry the tray in, I reached out to take it, thanking her and shutting the door as fast as I could without seeming suspicious.

My mother took the food before I could set it down, snatching up a piece of toast.

"How'd you know the kitchen would bring a tray?" I asked, frowning as my stomach rumbled softly. Normally this is what I would do, and I hadn't eaten much today. I wandered toward the window, away from the delicious smells, but they followed me. "How have you waited this long to eat but you're still able to shift? Did you have food stored somewhere?"

She laughed, holding up her hands in surrender at the volley of questions. She dusted off the breadcrumbs and picked up the fork, taking a bite of eggs before answering. "I have some insight into the castle patterns from back when I lived in the barracks with the rest of the Guard," she began.

That sparked a whole new set of questions in my mind, but she continued, "I don't have any remaining food stores, but I can usually shift at least a dozen times, if not more before things get desperate. Why do you ask? Is it different for you?"

Very different, I wanted to say. *I can only shift a handful of times at most before my Gift gives out.* I shrugged. "A little." Apparently my Gifting wasn't as strong as hers. At least, not yet. If that was the case, was there any limit to what she could do?

"Let's come back to the more important topic," she said, before I could ask anything else. "You want to stay."

My heart squeezed painfully in my chest.

I could only nod.

"Well then. What's your plan?"

I clenched my teeth. Wasn't it obvious? Crossing my arms, I turned to stare out at the gardens. "I had one, but thanks to you I don't anymore."

"You mean you don't have a *working* plan." Silverware scraped the plate as she tried to get every last bite.

My stomach clenched painfully. I wished she'd saved some for me. It'd look odd to request a second meal tray from the kitchens, which meant now I had to wait until tomorrow to eat.

Taking a deep breath, my mother dabbed her lips with the napkin. She pulled the desk chair out, then dragged it a little further into the corner, dropping into it with a contented sigh. "You have to put yourself in the *mind* of another Jinn, as well as their body. Think outside of what you would do, and ask what you would do as someone else."

"I wouldn't know where to start."

"Try. Picture yourself in the royal family's shoes—what would make you innocent in their eyes?"

I sighed. Just like when I was younger, she was relentless. It was a waste of time to argue. "They'd probably have to see another Jinni shift while I was in the same room, at the same time, in *this* form. Since they believe there's only one shape-shifter in the castle, that would prove my innocence." I shook my head, moving to sit on the bed. "It'll never happen. I'd need to touch someone else to shift them, and there's no way to do that without being seen. They'd figure it out."

"Mmm," she hummed, tilting her head, considering. "I'll admit it'd be difficult…"

"It'd be impossible," I said flatly, falling back on the mattress. I stared up at the silk canopy above.

Silence filled the room until curiosity made me prop myself up on my arms to look at her. She gazed at some spot over my shoulder, unseeing. After another long moment, she shook her head. "Perhaps you're right. What's another way you could claim to be innocent?"

"I could figure out this invisible mark they're putting on people and find a way to get it for myself," I said impulsively, thinking of Gabriel and how that would finally wipe the superior look off his face.

"It has potential." She smiled a little, the way she had when I'd tried to poison her. "I'm impressed." As my chest swelled a little at her praise, she added, "Unfortunately, it won't work. I'm fairly certain they're keeping track of who's marked."

I deflated. They'd be fools not to track the mark, and I knew she was right.

We were silent again.

Somehow, that was worse than her pushing me to search for solutions. It told me she didn't see an alternative either.

Though she'd never admit defeat, we both knew the Guard was slowly closing the trap with me inside it.

"Come with me instead," she spoke softly, confirming my guess. "We'll leave this place together."

"We can't," I reminded her with a half-hearted laugh. "The enchantment prevents everyone from leaving, have you not tested it? Unless you know something I don't?"

"Don't worry about that." Her face lit up, as if excited by the challenge.

I shook my head. She'd always been more optimistic than me. More willing to take risks. "I tried leaving in animal form already. It doesn't work. We can't leave, and we can't lift the enchantment."

Her laugh sounded like low bells. "Are you sure about that?"

Before I could answer, she began to shift. But not into a creature like I had… instead the queen of Jinn formed in front of my eyes, taking my mother's place.

My lips parted despite myself. "You'd dare to impersonate Queen Samaria?" I whispered.

"Guards!" she said in such a convincing tone that I jumped slightly. "We must lift the enchantment immediately, by order of the crown! The shifter was just spotted outside the castle, and they're escaping!"

I gaped at her. *Why didn't I think of that?* As she shifted back to her true form, I snapped my mouth shut. *Because I wouldn't have the nerve.*

My mother returned to her own form, picking up the cloth napkin as she sat down again, dabbing her lips as if this were normal dinner conversation instead of a life-changing option.

Possibly my *only* option at this point.

I couldn't deny that leaving was tempting.

After spending two months on the council, I didn't feel like I belonged here anymore than the day I'd arrived. Less, if that was possible.

Sighing, I crossed my arms. Shem's face appeared in my mind again along with a twinge of pain. If there was even the slightest chance, however improbable it seemed, I'd much rather stay. He was my one friend in the world. And I was lying to myself if I didn't wish he was more than that.

"Maybe we can discuss—" I began, when the wardrobe next to my mother made shuffling noises.

Someone had just traveled inside.

The door swung open.

15

SHEM'S GRINNING FACE APPEARED inside it. "I was able to get away after all, and I thought you might want company—are you talking to yourself?" he asked, stepping out and swinging around to glance at the corner where my mother sat.

I sucked in a breath.

But, of course, the corner was empty.

The speed of her shifting never failed to surprise me.

"I'm... practicing something I wanted to say to you," I said the first thing that came to mind. It was hard not to glance around the room and search for my mother.

"Oh?" He put his hands on his hips and faced me. "All right then, I'm ready."

"Ah," I fumbled for something to say, regretting my choice of words. "I need a bit more time to get my thoughts together."

"Take your time." He moved to lean against the wardrobe with a small smile.

Was I blushing? Normally I could stop that, but around him I got so flustered that I didn't notice in time.

He waited patiently.

I had to actually come up with something.

The silence lengthened, and under pressure I couldn't think. Swallowing, I opened my mouth, hoping something reasonable would come out, "Are you taking time to reassure all the ladies—" I winced at how jealous that sounded, "—council members, that is, individually?" I hoped he wouldn't notice.

Shem didn't smile for once. His serious gaze made my heart drop. "I haven't had a chance," he said quietly, stepping closer. "But I also don't have any desire to. I only wanted to see you."

I searched his eyes for meaning. He'd never been this forthright before. "Me?"

He swallowed and took one of my hands in his own. Was he nervous? "I find myself thinking about you often lately. Especially now, when everything seems so uncertain."

"Me?" I repeated again, feeling flustered. "Why?"

Blinking, he began to withdraw his hand. Was that hurt flickering in his eyes?

"I'm happy to hear that," I rushed to say, grasping his hand between my own. "Because…" I struggled to be as straightforward as him. "I've been thinking of you too."

"Have you?" The corners of his eyes creased as he smiled gently and squeezed my fingers. "I know you've been anxious about everything." He waved a hand in the air, gesturing to the castle as a whole. "The interviews are invasive, I'll admit, but they're quick and painless. This will all be over before you know it."

"I suppose it will be my turn soon," I whispered.

"It probably should be…" I glanced up at the smirk in his voice. "But I made sure your name was near the bottom of the list in the last fifty or so."

I bit my lip, unable my relief. "The others would hate it if they knew." Milcah and Jerusha in particular.

He grinned back. "They'd be livid."

A laugh slipped out as I pictured their reaction, but then my smile fell. This morning, he'd said the interviews should be over by the end of the day. The last bits of golden sunlight touched his face now, highlighting the evening shadow along Shem's jaw. It was almost the end of the day. It'd been a kind gesture, but it likely didn't buy me much more time. The Guard could still arrive any minute.

I stared at our hands. Neither of us had let go. I savored the small connection.

Lowering my voice, I murmured, "Does Gabriel know? Because he's stopped here multiple times already." Impulsively I added, "I don't want to suggest something that might cause more anxiety for the royal family, but… it almost makes me think he's hiding something. Why else would he be so persistent? Have the Guard members undergone interviews or are they considered above reproach?"

Slowly Shem pulled his hands from mine with a frown.

I shrugged, spreading my hands wide. "It's truly none of my business." Maybe I'd pushed too far. "I just thought you should know."

"I haven't noticed anything out of the

ordinary..." he trailed off, lips pressing together, glancing at the door.

I put my hand on his arm, feeling his pulse under my fingers. I waited until he met my gaze. "Just... maybe see if he has an alibi?" I asked softly, trying to sound uncertain. "Better to know if there's something to know..."

He nodded then, with a vacant look in his eyes. Shifting his stance, he refocused on me. "I'm sure you're right. I'll look into it."

Surprised that he gave in so easily, I hesitated, trying to think of something else to say while my mother was eavesdropping somewhere in the room. Now that he'd finally come here to see me, I hated that all I could think about was how I wanted him to leave.

"Thank you," I ended up saying lamely. "I appreciate it."

He slipped his fingers beneath mine once more, lacing them together. It felt natural. "Is there anything else I can do to make this time less difficult?"

I chewed on my lip. There was, in fact, something I wanted. I'd hoped for months now that it might happen naturally, but it never had. Now, for

THE SECRET SHADOW

all I knew, this might be my last chance. *So what if my mother sees?*

I threw caution to the wind. Stepping toward him quickly before I could lose my nerve, I tilted my face up, lifted onto my toes, and kissed him.

His lips were warm.

Eyes closed, I sank into him for a second, before realizing he hadn't moved.

Pulling back slightly, I looked at his full lips, reluctant to meet his eyes. Suddenly I was terrified that I'd made a mistake.

When he sucked in a breath, he confirmed it.

I'd gone too far.

Humiliation washed over me as I jerked away, unable to look at him.

Immediately his arms caught me, folding me back in. He gently lowered his face to mine. "Jezebel," he whispered.

And then he kissed me back.

Warmth chased the fears away and for a long moment I forgot everything else.

My shoulders relaxed as tension left my body, leaving me loose, almost giddy.

He brushed a hand over my cheek as he pulled back, tucking me into him and resting his chin on my head. Both of us breathed deeply, not saying anything. We didn't need to. The unexpected stillness was sweet.

"I should get back to the council or they'll wonder where I am," he said softly, as if this moment somehow required whispering. "But I'll come check on you as soon as I'm able to get away."

I only nodded. My voice would tremble if I tried to use it now.

He climbed back into the wardrobe, and closed the door. Through the tiny openings in the wooden carvings he was there one second and gone the next.

I let loose a heavy breath.

The wardrobe was empty. He was gone. It was what I'd wanted a few short minutes ago, except I didn't anymore.

I touched my lips. They were curved in an unconscious smile.

Shaking myself, I blinked to refocus and opened both wardrobe doors wide. This way no one could travel into it again until the doors were closed.

That would prevent any more surprises, no matter how sweet.

"Mother?" I whispered, turning to the corner where she'd last been.

Searching for the tiny stick creature, I found her

peeling away from the foot of the wardrobe where she'd blended in.

She grew to her full size in a few short breaths.

"Ah," she said softly once she could speak. "*Now* I understand why you're so insistent to stay." She strode over to the window, eyes on the gardens, or maybe on something only she could see. "I had something similar myself once."

"With father?" I asked.

She scoffed. "Not exactly. Your father... well, he helped me in many ways, but no. No, there was another here, in the Guard as well..."

She didn't finish the story, and I didn't know if I wanted to hear the details. They wouldn't change anything. In the end, she'd left, and that was all that mattered.

Turning away from the window, she faced me and sighed. "I might not have had to run if I'd had *that* particular Gift. Why haven't you used it yet? Are you saving it as a last resort?"

What? That didn't make any sense. She *did* have my shape-shifting Gift... This conversation felt like trying to untie an impossible knot.

I shook my head. "Are you saying you can't travel?" That was my only other Gift. That didn't make sense. *How does traveling help me in this situation?*

She only laughed. "You don't have to pretend with me, darling. I'm not going to turn you in. If I was, I would've done it already, don't you think?"

My head ached like it might split open. "Can you say it plainly? I'm not following."

"You really don't see it?" My mother frowned, gesturing toward the open wardrobe where Shem had last been. "You manipulated him so easily. Gifts like that usually take time to master and become so natural."

Manipulated?

"I would *never* manipulate Shem!" I yelled. Pulling back sharply, I glanced at the door, hoping no one was in the hall to overhear.

Grinding my fists against my eyes, I found them wet with tears I hadn't even noticed were falling. I drew in a ragged breath.

Technically, I *had* convinced Shem to do some things for me. But that was because he cared for me.

Wasn't it?

Little splinters bit into my fragile heart as my confidence wavered. I reached for the bed post beside me, needing to steady myself.

Had I used a Gift on him without realizing it?

I tried to remember our conversations. He'd agreed to help me avoid the interviews when the search first began. Had that been regular persuasion or something more? Milcah had been there! Surely she would've noticed a Gift like that being used and exposed it...

But then there was earlier today. He'd clearly wanted everyone to be available for interviews, and yet when I'd wished for an escape, he'd provided one.

A very private escape, no less...

No. I refused to believe it.

"Someone else maybe," I said in a firm, low voice, glaring at my mother. "But not Shem."

Someone else.

The words hit me as a face came to mind, unbidden. I wanted to deny it even as the reality sank in.

Gabriel.

I'd manipulated Gabriel.

There was no one in the castle who liked me *less,* besides him. Unlike Shem, he had no reason to listen to me. Yet he'd been determined to do the interview one moment and abandoned it a second later. After I'd told him to...

It was suspicious behavior all on its own, but

when added to all the rest, the evidence loomed large.

A tiny part of me allowed myself to consider it.

It would explain so much.

A chill snaked down my spine as I accepted the truth.

I have another Gift.

Trembling fingers lifted to my mouth. My hands were cold.

My mother studied my face, softening. "You truly didn't know, did you? You were so caught up in the chaos going on the last few days that you didn't recognize your own salvation was right under your nose."

I shook my head, tears in my eyes. The shock of it made me numb. "I knew it was possible for Jinn to get latent Gifts," I whispered. It was rare, but it could happen as late as age twenty-one. I was only eighteen. "I just thought that dormant Gifts all happened at the same time. After the shape-shifting, I thought that must be it for me…"

Gently, my mother took my hand. "Looks like you were wrong."

When I didn't respond, she reached out and tipped my chin up until I met her eyes. "Jezebel, this is an unparalleled Gift. It's not something to fear, but

THE SECRET SHADOW

to value."

She was wrong. It was another formidable Gift, yes, but that only made it another reason for Jinn to fear and renounce me.

"It must be powerful, for it to come to you so naturally," my mother added softly, letting go of my chin.

I cringed.

"Why does that upset you?"

A knock sounded on the door, startling both of us.

In an instant, my original problems came rushing back, reminding me that this new Gift wasn't my only concern. "That has to be the Guard," I said on a gasp. "It's time for my interview. What do I do?"

"Jezebel!" My mother took hold of my shoulders and shook me. "Think! This is the solution you've been looking for."

She meant manipulate the Guard.

That's treason.

Automatically I shook my head. "If they found out I used a Gift like this, especially to avoid a royal order, I'd be sentenced to death."

"Who's going to find out?" she pushed.

Knocking sounded again, louder this time. "Open up in the name of the king!"

"One minute!" I called out frantically. "I'm—I'm not decent!" My voice cracked, and I could only hope they'd listen.

"This is a much easier option than your plans to frame someone," my mother whispered now as she backed up to the wardrobe, stepping inside. "Convince them you're innocent and you'll get what you always wanted: the ability to stay here."

I'd have to be insane to consider what she suggested. It went against the first Unbreakable Law of Jinn: never use a Gift to deceive.

Could I truly use a Gift like this to my advantage, when it meant disobeying the royal family—including Shem?

Maybe.

If I could even figure out how to use the Gift in time.

Closing one of the wardrobe doors, my mother paused with her hand on the other, to look at me. "Unless you'd like to come with me? The offer still stands."

16

I WAS TEMPTED.

Evening light trickled in through the window as the sun set, casting everything in my room in gold. My lips still tingled from when Shem had kissed me. Inside the wardrobe, my mother waited, hand outstretched slightly.

I didn't want to lose any of this.

But I had to make a choice.

Turning my mother's words over in my head, a rising sense of hope filled me. Maybe she was right. This unexpected Gift was the impossible option I'd been searching for. It could allow me to stay after all.

"Your minute is almost up!" a gruff voice yelled from the other side of the door. It sounded familiar.

"If the interview goes poorly, I'll come with you," I whispered to my mother, taking a step back. "Hopefully, you can find me after."

She nodded, hearing what I left unspoken. If I wasn't here, she'd look for me in the dungeons.

With a soft click, she pulled the wardrobe closed. A second later, she vanished.

I started shaking.

Could my new Gift help me around the truth spell? What if I failed?

Convince them you're innocent.

Rushing to my attached bathing room, I hurried to splash water on my face.

My eyes were red and my skin blotchy. Staring into the mirror, I carefully shifted my features until I'd removed all evidence of my tears. It ate up precious seconds, taking far longer than it would've taken my mother. I was starving by the time I finished such detailed work, but it would do.

I wished I'd had a chance to practice this new Gift—to use it intentionally at least once before I had to use it to save my own life.

THE SECRET SHADOW

A heavy hand banged on the door again. "By order of the King and Queen of Jinn, if this door does not open soon I'm commanded to—"

"Yes?" I swung it open before the guard could finish.

It was Gabriel.

Of course it was.

A female Guard named Kinah stood beside him.

Anyone else would've been better—

No, I stopped my train of thought and smiled. *He will be perfect.* I'd have no qualms about testing out this Gift on him. No guilt to distract me.

I took a step back and wordlessly waved them in.

Gabriel strode inside, eyes sweeping the room, while Kinah went straight to my little desk with a small case and set it down beside my glass jar.

The hair on the back of my neck rose at the sight of it.

Unclasping the lock, she opened the lid to reveal ingredients for what I suspected was the infamous truth spell. She poured a cup of water and began to mix in different ingredients, making the liquid change from clear to a muddy brown with a hint of blue.

I stood by the open door, unable to swallow.

This may have been a huge mistake.

Glancing at my wardrobe, I almost made a run for it.

What if I can't make the Gift work on demand?

There was no room for error, and I had no idea how or where to start.

Gabriel paused in his search of the room to glance back at me, and I finally remembered to close the door.

It was like closing myself into my own tomb.

Forcing a swallow, I cleared my throat and moved closer to Gabriel. *Do I need proximity? What if it doesn't work on both of them at once, and I tip the other off?*

Questions surged as I stood there blinking.

Gabriel frowned and crossed his arms, making his armor clink together. "Have a seat on the bed."

I did as he asked, struggling to figure out my new Gift before it was too late. Something that Kinah wouldn't find suspicious if it didn't affect her in the same way…

"There's no need to hurry," I tried, attempting a trembling smile.

Gabriel's stern features didn't change in the slightest. He merely looked down his nose at me. I

THE SECRET SHADOW

bit back the urge to shift Gabriel into a little bug and see how self-important he was then.

"Ready," Kinah said behind him.

He turned to take the cup from her.

Icy panic gripped me.

Before I realized it, I was standing, tensed to run.

"Remain seated," Gabriel snapped, fingers tightening around his crystal spear.

I'd never make it to the wardrobe.

Unconsciously, I placed my hand over where he gripped his weapon. "It's okay," I said urgently, trying to convince him for real now—Gift or no Gift. "I'm not a threat."

Behind him, Kinah glanced up from where she'd been putting away the remains of the enchantment ingredients. Her eyes met mine, then darted to Gabriel. Apparently, she didn't find anything to be concerned about, because she turned back to the box.

I dared another glance at Gabriel.

He hadn't moved.

Beneath my fingers, though, his hand had relaxed on the weapon.

Had it worked?

When I raised my gaze to his, I recognized the slightly vacant look.

It seemed like it.

If that were the case, then it seemed like I needed to touch him for the manipulation to take effect, at least for now. I disliked how limiting that made the Gift. Hopefully it might develop into something stronger in the future…

I didn't have time to consider it further.

"Drink," Gabriel said, holding out the cup to me.

I couldn't.

But I couldn't say no either.

"Of course," I said, as calmly as possible, reaching for the cup.

Kinah would join him any second now. I needed to move quickly.

Here was the true test.

I held Gabriel's gaze as I wrapped my hand around the cup, making sure to also touch his fingers. Quickly, without breaking eye contact, I whispered the same word back to him, "Drink."

I spoke so softly I worried he wouldn't hear me, or that Kinah *would*.

He lifted the cup obediently.

Once again Kinah paused in her work, turning to check on us.

I caught Gabriel's wrist before he reached his lips, preventing him from tilting his head back and giving us away. He stared at me, and I held his gaze, terrified that breaking it might decrease my control over him.

She couldn't see our silent exchange, but in the corner of my vision she frowned slightly. Then she shrugged and turned back to the case.

As soon as her gaze left us, I let go.

He drank.

I took the cup back from him, keeping my hand firmly around his wrist.

Eyes still locked with his, I spoke louder now, for Kinah to hear. "It's done." And then in case that wasn't specific enough, I added for good measure, specifically to Gabriel, "I drank all of it."

Watching both of them carefully for any sign they weren't convinced, I slowly let go and waited.

Gabriel crossed his arms and nodded, seeming to return to his usual arrogant self. "Have a seat and get comfortable. We have some questions for you."

Easing myself back onto the bed, I tried to appear relaxed and confident. As long as neither of them became aware of what I'd done, the worst of the interview was behind me—I hoped.

Gabriel turned to drag the desk chair across the floor, making me wince at the sound. He slammed it down to sit in front of me.

Kinah closed the lid of her case with a light snap and came to stand behind him.

They were close, but not close enough for me to touch. Which meant I'd have to finish the rest of this interview without my manipulation.

Hopefully I'd done enough.

"You should begin to feel the effects of the truth spell soon," Gabriel began in a flat tone, as if he'd said this a hundred times before. "You may feel a bit light-headed. And you'll find that fighting against the desire to tell the truth will make you physically ill."

That's when I knew for sure.

It'd worked.

Gabriel hated me as much as I loathed him. Ever since I'd come to the castle I'd stumbled through the court etiquette, offending him and the rest of the Guard constantly. I was no one, yet I'd been elevated to a status above his own, and he'd never forgotten the slight.

Gabriel would never willingly go along with my ruse. Which meant he truly believed I'd drank the cup dry.

I'd made him believe it.

Convince them, my mother's words came back

to me, and hope freed my tense muscles, allowing my shoulders to sag and my clenched hands to loosen. I couldn't help smiling slightly. She'd known what I could do. "I'm ready whenever you are."

"We've already begun," Gabriel snapped, crossing his arms. He tilted slightly to one side before he caught himself, blinking.

The light-headedness. I held back another smile.

Frowning, he rubbed his brow slightly and said, "Tell us your full name."

"Jezebel, daughter of Sariah, daughter of Aziza," I whispered, feeling exposed, though this particular truth wasn't what they'd come here for. Had my mother returned to the room? Was she here now, watching? More importantly, did anyone still know her from the past that might recognize my family name?

It didn't seem so. Gabriel continued without pause, although he did seem to be blinking more than usual. "Now, tell us your name is Queen Samaria."

I opened my mouth obediently, barely catching myself. Instead of speaking, I made a show of clutching my stomach, hunching over as if in pain. "I… can't," I said finally, peeking up at them beneath my lashes, hoping this was a typical reaction. If they'd lied about how the spell worked, I'd know soon.

"Don't push yourself," Gabriel said, though he'd certainly waited long enough, letting me experience the supposed pain. He pulled out a small booklet, tearing out a piece of paper and handing it to Kinah.

She moved to my desk to write, although she was forced to stand since Gabriel had taken the only chair.

"Let's move on," he continued. "Tell us your Gifts, starting with the least important and moving to the most important. Don't leave any out."

I tried not to gape at the invasiveness of the question. *This* was how they chose to go about finding the shifter? Not, "Do you have a shifting ability?" or "Are you Gifted with changing shape?" but instead they were gathering a full list of every single castle inhabitant's Gifts?

Gifts were incredibly personal.

Some Jinn preferred not to share theirs with anyone, and that had always been our right. No one should be forced to reveal something so private.

And yet, here we were.

They'd have record of every Gift in the castle by the time this was over.

It made my blood boil.

THE SECRET SHADOW

Kinah had dipped her pen in the ink pot and now held it hovered over the paper, waiting.

Seated across from me, Gabriel kept his features still, hiding most emotion, but I could've sworn a small smirk touched his lips. "Resisting the urge to tell us will only prolong the interview, and as a result, your discomfort," he said after a long moment passed. "The king and queen require this information, but it will not be shared with the general public."

As if that made it acceptable.

At least, since he'd made that declaration without difficulty after taking the potion, I knew he was speaking the truth.

Eyes narrowing, I hoped it was normal for those under the truth spell to be furious, because I couldn't hide my disgust. "Traveling," I spat.

Nodding, he turned to Kinah and waved for her to write it down.

The sound of pen scratching against paper was the only sound in the room.

Once done, the silence stretched louder than ever.

"Continue," Gabriel said, eyes pinned on me.

How long did my newly discovered Gift last? Did it convince him permanently or would he start to have doubts?

"That's it," I replied, crossing my arms and lifting my chin. Though I pretended calm, my whole body tensed. If I needed to, maybe I could lean forward to touch him again for my Gift to work. Would Kinah notice? I'd have to be quick...

He squinted at me. "That's all?"

Does he not believe me?

I bit my tongue, barely managing to keep my face void of emotion. Subtly, I leaned forward, ready to spring.

"Can you repeat that?"

I ground my teeth together. He wasn't questioning out of disbelief—he was trying to humble me.

"My *only* Gift is traveling," I growled. Even though it wasn't true, my pride smarted.

He let out a short contemptuous laugh. "Does the prince know? I would've thought—" he paused, wincing as if whatever he'd been about to say was causing him physical pain. After drawing a deep breath, he said instead, "—I always thought council members were supposed to be skilled."

I flushed hot from head to toe, shaking. Not from fear anymore, but pure, scorching fury.

THE SECRET SHADOW

I should use my Gift to make him strip naked and stroll through the castle halls. Or better yet, maybe I should reconsider framing someone, and frame *him*.

Another chuckle slipped out as he shook his head. Standing, he brought the chair back to the desk, where Kinah blew on the ink to dry it before handing him the paper. He added it to the little book, which he then tucked into a pocket beneath his armored breastplate. I took solace in the way he seemed paler than usual and swayed as if dizzy.

Once again his voice returned to the monotone of repetition, "Thank you for your cooperation. The crown will let you know when circumstances change and the threat is neutralized."

It's over? I succeeded?

If traveling really *had* been my only Gift, I'd have been terribly offended that I'd been forced to reveal that, so I tried not to let my excitement show as I stood too.

I can't believe it worked.

Kinah pulled a royal signet from her pocket, meant to seal a letter. It was dry.

Without warning, she placed it on my forehead, pressing, as if there were truly ink there.

I tried not to frown.

She removed the seal, inspecting her work.

My hand itched to touch my brow. I couldn't feel a thing.

At my expression, she held up the signet briefly. "It's enchanted. The Guard will see you're marked and it will prevent multiple, unnecessary interviews."

The mark.

I blew out a breath of relief.

If I'd known it was that easy, I might've tried to steal the signet and simply mark myself instead.

I nodded understanding, moving to open the door for them.

All that mattered was that they'd believed me.

As Gabriel exited and Kinah followed, I couldn't resist saying, "I'm so glad the interview went well, and that I was proven *innocent*."

I emphasized the last word. Gabriel's lips turned down in annoyance as he reached in to take the door handle and yanked it shut.

Blowing out a heavy breath, I sagged back against the wall, exhausted.

That could've gone horribly wrong.

I smiled, turning away from the door. My eyes caught on the wardrobe.

THE SECRET SHADOW

On the eyes within.

Pale blue and familiar.

Staring out at me.

I would know those eyes anywhere.

Shem.

17

"HOW LONG HAVE YOU been there?" My voice shook.

More importantly, how much had he seen?

He swung the wardrobe door open slowly on silent hinges. The dresses swished softly as he brushed past them and stepped out.

For a long minute, he didn't speak. I'd never seen him stare at me so coldly before. "You used a Gift on the Guard."

I opened my mouth, but nothing came out. To deny it would only make it worse.

"You forced him to drink the elixir instead of you," he whispered.

I winced.

Now I knew how much he'd seen.

Forced was a much harsher word than convince.

But I couldn't deny it.

"Did you use this Gift of manipulation on me as well?" he asked, dragging his eyes from the door back to mine. The hurt and betrayal in them brought tears to my eyes.

This is what I'd feared most. Why I'd never gotten the nerve to tell him my secrets. I deserved his hatred.

"Not intentionally…" I closed my eyes so I couldn't see the horror on his face. "I am so sorry. I didn't know that I was doing it. I—it was only an hour ago that I learned of its existence, I swear to you."

When he didn't immediately reply, I risked a glance at him.

He stood rigid with his hands clenched at his sides. "So," he finally replied. "You knew of it when the interview began."

My stomach dropped.

"Meaning, you knowingly used a Gift against the Jinni Guard in an interview—"

"Not against them!" I protested. "I just wanted to protect myself."

"Does that mean you are the shape-shifter as well?" he spoke over me.

I couldn't speak.

He looked stricken.

For a long moment, neither of us spoke, until finally, he whispered, "I suppose I must take that as a yes."

"Not—" my voice sounded strangled. I cleared my throat and tried again. "Not the one they're looking for."

Rearing back, Shem paled further. "There are others?"

I winced. "As far as I know, just one other. You have to believe me."

"I don't have to do anything," he said in a dark tone, stepping back without ever taking his eyes off me.

"Shem," I pleaded with him. But when I took a step toward him, he took two more back, moving too fast toward the wardrobe.

"Please," I stopped, holding my hands out in surrender, whispering through the tears. "You can trust me. You *know* me."

He put one foot in the wardrobe, hesitating. Lifting his eyes to my face, he whispered, "Do I?"

That struck me like a blow.

"I've been here for months now. I've never—" my voice shook so hard that I couldn't speak. Swallowing I tried again. "I've *never* used any of my Gifts against you."

He stood as still as a statue. One foot was still in the wardrobe, and his scowl was pinned to a spot on the floor.

"I don't know how to prove myself," I said through the tears sliding down my cheeks. My voice was thick with them. "Except to promise you on my life that I would never hurt you."

"And yet you already did." The wardrobe door cracked shut between us, punctuating his words. It hit so hard that it bounced back open, revealing an empty wardrobe, besides the few dresses that hung inside.

Sobbing, I crumpled to the floor.

I couldn't chase him. He'd only fear me more and likely call the Guard. Maybe he was calling them now.

I didn't move.

If he did turn me in, I deserved it. It was my fault he'd found out this way. No, more than that, it was my fault he didn't trust me, because without realizing it, I'd used my new Gift on him more than once.

Looking back at the last few days, I brought a shaking hand to my lips.

Possibly many times.

Burying my face in my knees, I let the tears come.

He called it manipulation, the same word my mother had used that I'd despised. And he was right.

If he hated me, it was only fair.

I tried to pull myself together, to hide my anguish, in case my mother came back. But I couldn't stop the flood of tears. I'd never admitted to myself how much I'd come to care for Shem. And now I'd ruined everything.

He'd never forgive me.

Swiping at the wetness on my cheeks, I yanked myself to my feet. I could *make* him forgive me…

I shook my head, ashamed that I would even consider it. Sinking onto the bed, I fell back on it, staring up at the canopy.

Was there any other way to salvage this?

I desperately wanted to avoid repeating past mistakes.

I wanted to be the good, noble, innocent Jinni

girl that Shem had thought I was.

What would *that* girl do?

It was tempting to chase after Shem and figure it out later, but some part of me knew that would end in disaster. If I was to win his trust back, I needed to somehow come clean. It was a paradox. Because it was too late—wasn't it?

Maybe there was another way to prove that I could be trusted.

I bit my lip, considering.

I could tell his parents.

My heart dropped just thinking about it, and there was a good chance it wouldn't work…

But how else could I show Shem that I was on his side?

Jumping off the bed, I took a few precious seconds in the bathing room to dry my face and pull myself together, before I stepped into the wardrobe to travel.

I took a deep breath and fresh tears came to my eyes. Shem's unique scent of cinnamon and pine still hung in the air. My hand brushed against something, and for a second I could've sworn it was a hand, but the wardrobe was empty. My mind was creating a phantom touch, wishing he was still there.

My fingers shook, despite my resolve, as I took

the knob and pulled the door closed behind me.

This could either go really well or horribly wrong.

So far, every single one of my plans had been the latter.

But there was only one way to find out.

18

I TRAVELED TO THE royal chambers. Or rather, to the entrance on the east side of the castle. Before I could stride down the long hallways to the royal family, I had to get past this checkpoint first.

Six guards stood watch.

Which meant six crystal spears were pointed at my face.

I attempted to appear calm as I swallowed, hard.

An icy wave flashed across my skin, and my ears felt like they might pop. The sensation of being in a bubble flooded my whole body, then swept away as

I forced myself to focus.

I was going to turn myself in.

This is for Shem.

I pointed wordlessly to the mark on my forehead, mouth so dry that I had to swallow twice more before I could speak. "I've been cleared."

The guards exchanged glances. They didn't lower their weapons immediately, but one stepped forward to touch my brow. It tingled under the touch, responding. Some of the tension in the air faded at whatever they saw. "Business?"

That part of me that always whispered to use my Gifts reared its head again, but I shoved it down. It was time to be honest. This is what I should've done all along. This is what Shem would want me to do. It might very well be my downfall, but at least he'd see that I'd tried.

Gathering my nerve, I took a deep breath. "I have urgent news for the king and queen."

"It's not a good time," the lead guard said. "Give us the message, and we'll see they receive it."

I shook my head. "No," I croaked, clearing my throat. Pressing my shoulders back to project a confidence I didn't feel, I said, "It's about the shape-shifter. They need to hear it from me."

He broke his stern façade to glance at the other guards. If I lied, he'd be responsible. But if my claim was true, turning me away could anger the royal family. Most of them knew I was on the prince's council, which I hoped would work in my favor.

Finally, he nodded. "Come with me."

He nodded to the female Jinni beside him, who took over pointing a weapon in my face. They led me down the hall to a large meeting room between the king and queen's chambers. He knocked, then entered, shutting the door behind him.

Standing in the hushed hallway, surrounded by the other guards, I focused on my breathing which had grown shallow, and rehearsed what I would say.

Once again, I could've sworn I smelled the sweet fragrance of cinnamon and wood. A breeze blew across the back of my neck like a breath. My skin prickled. When I glanced around, no one else was there.

One of the guards frowned at me.

I stopped fidgeting.

The door opened after another long minute. "They'll see you," the first guard said, with narrowed eyes.

Smiling sweetly, I enjoyed the small victory. Halfway through the door, he shoved me forward, making me trip slightly, and both guards followed me in.

It wasn't the grand entrance I'd hoped for.

King Jubal and Queen Samaria sat on the soft green sofa straight ahead. The queen held her teacup paused halfway to her lips. Impatiently, the king gestured for me to come forward. "We accepted your request for our son's sake," he said briskly, by way of a greeting. "But be quick about it. Why are you here?"

Why was I here?

"I—" The guards shut the door behind me with a loud thunk and all my flowery practiced words flew out of my head. He wanted me to be quick. And Shem would want me to be honest. Best to get to the heart of it, then. Swallowing hard, I said, "I've come to tell you the truth."

Frowning, Samaria lowered her teacup, setting it down on the small table beside her.

I pressed on, hoping I'd somehow say the right thing. "I made a discovery, only an hour or so ago, that I have a new Gift."

It wasn't unusual for someone my age to continue developing Gifts.

They both nodded understanding, watching me

THE SECRET SHADOW

warily. "Is this relevant to the crown?" the king asked when I didn't immediately continue.

"It is," I managed to say, clasping my hands in front of me where I'd been wringing them. *Stay calm. Make them trust you.* "As you know, I could keep this Gift to myself, but out of loyalty to the crown—and to your son—" I added, wishing Shem could hear and know how much I meant it, "—I feel it's important for you to know."

My fingers refused to stay still. Bringing my hands behind my back where they wouldn't be seen, I tried to stand tall and project confidence. "Before I share with you what the Gift is, I want to make it clear that I believe it can be of enormous value to you."

Their flat expressions didn't change.

I was tempted to draw a bit closer. Close enough to take their hands and use my new Gift on them, to help persuade them to my cause.

Just a tiny push.

No. I took a deep breath and blew it out. *That wouldn't be true honor. Shem would only think worse of me.*

The king's foot tapped irritably.

"I think this new Gift could make me a powerful ally for you. I can help you track down the shifter you've been looking for."

"How so?" the queen asked.

At the same time, the king leaned forward suspiciously. "What is your new Gift? Tell us immediately."

Though it was risky to disobey, I said instead, "I must beg you not to tell anyone else. It would break my heart to be feared for no reason, when I would never harm anyone." For good measure, I bowed my head. Using my Gift, I formed a tear and let it trickle down my cheek.

They sat stoically, unconvinced.

I dropped to my knees, abandoning self-respect to truly beg now. The tears that followed were real. "Please," I said in a voice barely above a whisper. "Let me work for you and use my Gifts on behalf of the crown. I want nothing more than to help. I'll do anything."

When I dared to glance up, the king and queen were exchanging a look I couldn't read.

"Get up," the queen said finally, with some compassion. She waved for me to sit across from them. "You can trust us to react calmly. Tell us now, what is this new Gift that's causing such fear?"

As I lowered myself onto the soft sofa, I turned

THE SECRET SHADOW

to look over my shoulder at the guards standing by the door. "Please don't make me tell you in front of them." I dropped my gaze to my hands. "It would spread through the castle in less than an hour. And," I added, "Once it's made known, it won't be nearly as helpful to the crown."

The king raised a single brow, intrigued now. He waved a hand at the guards. "Go back outside. We'll call if we need you." Clearly, he didn't find me much of a threat, despite how I'd described my ability.

Waiting until the guards slowly turned and left, closing the door behind them, I sucked in another breath.

I still couldn't find the courage.

"You can restrain me, if that will prove my loyalty," I said, holding my hands out in front of me, hoping they wouldn't notice I'd said this only after the guards left.

"It won't be necessary, child," the king said gruffly. "Now. Out with it. Don't make us wait any longer."

I cleared my throat and nodded. My mind spun wildly as I tried to decide where to start. Perhaps before I shared my newest Gift, I needed to share the one that had caused me so much heartache from the start. "It's... multiple Gifts, really. But the most important thing you should know is that, while I am *not* the shape-shifter who is threatening this castle… I do have a slight shape-shifting ability."

I tried to minimize my strength in the Gift, but still winced as I said it.

The words could never be taken back now.

The queen stiffened, gripping her skirts as her eyes grew wide, though to her credit she did attempt to remain calm as she'd promised.

The king, on the other hand, did not, roaring, "What?"

I tried to curl inward and seem as small as possible. "Please, hear me out." I brought my hands together in supplication. "I think—I might be able to help you find the other shape-shifter, or at least, serve as one in the Guard?"

"We would not allow a known shape-shifter to be in the Guard," the queen said, putting a horrified hand to her chest.

But the king paused.

Staring at me for a long moment, he tipped his head, seeming to consider it.

The only sound in the room was the tick of the clock on the mantel.

At the risk of digging an even deeper hole—it

couldn't get much worse now—I spoke up, "I can become both animal, human, and Jinni..." That seemed to make them tense, and I tried to backtrack. "Truthfully only animals come naturally to me, but in animal form I could make a valuable spy—"

"We cannot," Samaria hissed to her husband, interrupting me. "Not after what happened last time."

His voice was a low rumble as he finally spoke, "If, as she said, my dear, her secret is *not* known..." He ran a hand over his carefully trimmed beard. "There is some truth to her claims. It *could* be very useful to have someone with her skills working for us."

"I'll do whatever you ask of me," I promised, lifting my gaze to his. "If I ever fail you, you may have my Gifts severed."

Of course, they didn't actually need my permission for a Severance. If I ever crossed them, or if they simply decided not to trust me, that's exactly what I'd be sentenced to.

Still, it might help my case to offer.

A Severance was the most severe penalty in Jinn. Far worse than even death. To have your Gifts severed meant a miserable existence with a slow, agonizing decline until eventually one couldn't stand the pain anymore.

Instead of answering, the king paused, lifting his eyes to the wall behind me.

Shem's voice came from the same place, "You're attempting to manipulate my parents with your lies as well?"

Eyes wide, I spun to face him. *Where did he come from?* "No, of course not!"

He stood only a few steps away. There was no furniture nearby to hide behind. And I hadn't heard the door open... *Has he been here all along?* For a split second, I wondered if he had a secret Gift of his own?

"You didn't give me a chance to explain," I said softly, almost forgetting his parents were listening.

Shem's gaze lifted over my head, to his father's. He strode around the sofa, giving me a wide berth, coming to stand beside his parents. In a hard tone, he told them, "You really shouldn't have sent the guard into the hall."

King Jubal sighed. "Don't be overly dramatic. You know we each have protections in place for shifters." His hand strayed unconsciously to the large ruby nestled among a dozen other jewels in the center of his ornamental armor.

Enchanted in some way, most likely. How he

thought it protected him from shifters, however, I couldn't say, since it hadn't seemed to respond to me in the slightest.

I kept my mouth shut.

"We already know about her Gift," the queen said, placing a soothing hand over Shem's on her arm. "She told us everything."

Well, not everything, I thought, wondering if I should speak up about that now or later. I hadn't had a chance to finish sharing my other dangerous Gift. Odds were good they'd like it even less than they liked shape-shifting, but perhaps they'd also see it as useful.

Before they could argue further, I pressed my hands together and repeated, "I would *never* hurt you or your family. I'm loyal to the crown. I've already told your parents that I'm here to serve, whether they want to expose my Gift, or…" I paused, hoping for the second option. "If they want to use my Gift in secret. Either way, I'm a humble servant."

Though still seated on the sofa, I bowed my upper body and kept my head down, terrified to look at Shem's face. Tears filled my eyes as I pictured the fear and distrust from earlier. Or had it been disgust?

If he still felt that way, even after my risking everything to tell the truth, I couldn't bear it.

I waited for him to speak now and twist his parent's view of me, to tell them of my *other* equally threatening Gift. But he was silent.

"I would never hurt any of you," I whispered to the floor, when the quiet stretched longer than I could bear.

If my eyes hadn't been trained on my feet, I wouldn't have noticed it.

A tiny creature on the ground.

Slowly, it peeled away from the wooden leg of the sofa. It waved a tiny twig-like arm up at me.

A walking stick.

Mother.

19

NO! I WANTED TO scream as she began to shape-shift.

But I couldn't without giving myself away.

Instead, I gaped from my chair as she exploded into the room, filling it in a few short breaths, shifting until her body reached all the way to the high ceiling.

In the form of a dragon.

She winked one oval, predatory eye. As her neck hit the plaster above, making it rain down on us, her razor sharp claws knocked down the blockade beside the door making it drop into place, locking us in. She fell onto all fours with a crash, claws making deep gouges in the floor.

I was still seated on the couch, too stunned to move.

Each time I thought my mother might finally care about me, she proved me wrong. She *knew* how badly I wanted to stay, and yet she seemed determined to ruin it. I didn't even know why I was surprised anymore.

Her red scales shimmered over huge, muscled thighs. Her long tail swung toward my face.

I ducked.

I'd never encountered a dragon in real life, so I'd never had the opportunity to try this shift—or even to think of it—but clearly my mother had.

Shem and his parents leapt back from their sofa, scrambling to retreat as she turned to roar at them.

Their mouths were open in silent screams—or maybe not silent, and I just couldn't hear over my mother's roar and the blood rushing into my ears.

The queen trembled, seeming unable to react or use whatever Gifts she might have. Perhaps her Gifts were useless against a beast. But King Jubal reacted immediately. He spread his hands in front of him, creating a wall of fire. It roared to life in a heartbeat.

THE SECRET SHADOW

This was the kind of Gift most Jinn feared.

Unfortunately, it did next to nothing against a dragon.

A growl ripped from my mother's throat as she side-swiped a heavy table with her tail, sending it crashing against the door and stepped right through the king's wall of fire.

Shem stood stunned into inaction.

I launched out of my chair finally, moving toward him on instinct. "Don't you dare hurt him!" I screamed, adding silently, *If you do, I'll never forgive you!*

Queen Samaria screamed and turned to run, trying to drag Shem with her, while the king yelled for the guards. Why weren't they answering?

Thudding noises against the main door registered faintly in the back of my mind. They were certainly trying.

King Jubal yanked a ceremonial sword from where it hung on the wall and stood in front of his wife, with only the dull blade and his decorative armor, prepared to fight the beast.

My mother lowered her head, eyes pinning them in place, stalking them.

Unhinging her jaw, she bared her teeth.

Heavy breaths in and out stoked the fire

blooming in her chest, visible through her scales. Smoke began to pour from her open mouth.

She wouldn't.

"Stop!" I screamed again.

She didn't listen.

I dodged in front of the royal family, daring to put myself between them and her. "Don't hurt them!" I pleaded with her, silently begging her not to take this away from me too.

She was about to set my last chance to stay in the castle on fire.

Maybe that was why she was doing this.

She thrust me aside, talons scraping my skin and tearing my clothes, as her yellow eyes never left the royals. Rearing back, her head hit the high ceiling. Another roar made the furniture shake.

Tears sprung to my eyes—she was going to incinerate them!

I leapt forward.

Shifting faster than I'd thought possible, I copied her dragon form—the muscles, scales, fangs, and most importantly, the fire.

The dragon form was surprisingly similar to my favorite lizard form. I made my scales deep green like I always did. That way Shem would know it was me—I hoped.

Using my powerful wings, I shoved her back, forcing her to give ground and shielding the royals with my body.

Once again, she unhinged her jaw and smoke poured out, warning me of what was coming.

Flames blasted me back.

I screamed.

In my dragon form, it came out as a screeching roar.

It shouldn't have even stung. But I'd never seen a dragon's scales before this moment, and I hadn't imitated them as well as I'd thought.

My left wing and shoulder had taken the brunt of the burn.

Limping, I held my wing at an odd angle and swung around, using my huge tail to knock her off her feet.

My heavy body slammed into Shem by accident.

I winced as he fell back a few steps.

I hadn't meant to do that.

A roar behind me was my only warning before her body crashed into mine.

It was a surprisingly light hit.

My feet clawed deep slices in the floor as I slid back, but I barely felt the impact. Instead, I felt the king's body bouncing off mine. He was flung back against the wall, where he sagged as he slumped down. Out cold.

Shem and his mother grabbed him by the arms, dragging him out of the way.

I stamped my feet and growled fiercely at the other dragon.

Was it my mother?

I wasn't sure anymore. I couldn't fathom why she'd do this.

Head lowering, haunches tensing to leap, I bared my teeth at her and snarled.

Either way, I was done holding back.

"Guards!" Shem yelled over the rumbles in our throats. The other dragon and I began to circle each other, each huffing breaths to stoke our fires.

He didn't bother to yell after that. It was useless, and he knew it. The guards were on the other side of a heavily enchanted door meant to protect the most important Jinn in the floating islands. Those spells wouldn't be broken quickly.

He and his mother hurried to barricade themselves and the king in the bathing room. As the door swung shut, I caught a glimpse of the king lying prone on the tiles behind them, not moving. The white tiles had a long streak of dark red.

Heavy pounding filled the air as the guards continued to attack the enchanted wood. It splintered and cracked. But thanks to the magic meant to protect the royal family, it held strong.

Muffled voices argued. Probably quarreling over whether they could use a Gift to burst through without harming a royal by accident.

The dragon attacked while I was distracted.

Throwing her whole weight against me, she tackled me to the ground, bending my injured wing at a sharp angle.

I gave a strangled roar.

She came at me once more before I could find my footing, throwing me back, almost as if she were trying to push me away from the royals.

I swung wildly with my claws and attempted to breathe fire.

Only a huff of hot air came out.

Another sharp scratch against my—unfortunately very penetrable—scales, and I fell back.

Crashing through the door frame, I created a much larger hole in the wall as I stumbled into the adjoining room.

It was a bedroom, and it was much smaller.

Despite the tall ceilings, we barely fit, but she forced her way in after me anyway, teeth bared.

I braced for another attack.

With a roar, she flung herself upward instead, away from me, bursting through the ceiling above.

I gaped at the hole she'd created. The damage lay all around me, but her tail disappeared through the opening and heavy footsteps sounded above.

None of this made sense.

The footsteps grew lighter.

Was she back in her Jinni form? Or was she another creature now?

Meanwhile, crystal spears slammed against the door in the next room. Enchanted with power, meant to take down anything, they were thwarted by their own spells protecting the door from intruders, but they were slowly breaking through.

It shouldn't be long now.

I heard a soft click in the other room. Was Shem peeking out through the crack? Was he headed this way? My mother hadn't gone far, and Shem could easily get himself killed if I didn't figure out how to face her.

I gathered my haunches beneath me.

Launching myself upward, I landed in the dark,

THE SECRET SHADOW

unknown room above.

It was filled with shelves and tables, covered in objects of all shapes and sizes.

It took me a moment to recognize the space.

The last time I'd been here, Shem had brought me through that ornate, blue door fortified with iron locks and spells: we were in the vault for enchanted objects.

My mother's entrance had toppled one of the larger tables, and it now lay with the mahogany wood cracked in half, ruining the delicate designs carved all around the edges.

And it *was* my mother.

She crouched over the mess in her true form.

I'd thought it couldn't really be her, or that somehow she'd been forced to act the way she did, but she appeared relaxed, as if she'd already forgotten the battle below.

Fury rippled through my whole body.

The fire that I'd struggled to find finally ignited in my belly with a dull roar.

How could she do this to me?

I stayed in my dragon form, not trusting her in the slightest, and not at all sure what she was doing. Lowering my long neck to her eye level, I let a rumbling growl rip through me.

She ignored me.

I blinked.

Had she not *just* attacked me mere moments ago? Had I imagined the whole thing? I tried to make this scene mesh with the one from downstairs, and my head started to throb. *What's going on?*

She was sorting through the objects on the floor, keeping most of them. Her pockets were bulging as if she'd already gathered quite a bit. Glancing around, she murmured, "I need a satchel."

The pounding below didn't seem to touch her concentration as she found a nearby bag that apparently suited her needs.

"You're looming, Jezebel," she said when I wafted smoke in her direction.

I desperately wanted to ask *what in the name of Jinn* she was doing, but of course, I couldn't speak in this form.

Hesitating, I slowly shifted back to myself. As I did, a bone-deep exhaustion stole over me. I couldn't match her frequent shifts without time and food to regain my energy. If she attacked me again, I didn't know if I could shift fast enough to fight back.

But she didn't *seem* hostile.

I frowned, sagging against the side of the broken

table. My wounded arm dangled uselessly at my side. Shock had kept the pain at bay, but sharp stabs grew stronger by the second, making me cradle the limb gently. The room spun. I sucked in a deep breath, and tried to focus. "Have you lost your mind?"

Below a heavy table scraped across the floor. The banging on the door renewed but with the crackle of wood splintered after each hit now, as if it was finally beginning to break. Was the enchantment on the lock broken?

I tensed, turning to the hole in the floor.

We had maybe another minute if we were lucky, and if the guards chose to approach with caution.

"We don't have much time," she murmured, still sorting through the objects on the shelves around the room. "I have to make it count."

A small knife, a handheld mirror, and an ink pot, all went into the large linen bag.

Finally, she glanced up. "I thought if you were intent on staying here that we should make it look good, darling."

Dozens of Kathenoths were stacked neatly on shelves along one wall. She passed over those.

My mouth hung slightly open. "Are you trying to justify what you did? By saying you somehow did it for me?" I shook my head. That seemed far-fetched, even for her. "They're going to be here any minute. I'm sure I *will* stay here now—in the dungeons, thanks to you."

On another table, she sorted through a variety of household objects, as if she hadn't even heard me. Adding a few to her bag, she paused on a spindle. It belonged to a spinning wheel, though only the top piece was here in the room. She ran a finger up the length of it, contemplatively, though she avoided the sharp tip. Just when I thought she wasn't going to answer, she murmured, "You want them to trust you, don't you?"

"They *do* trust me," I snapped, cradling my injured arm where the burn was beginning to make me shiver as the pain set in. "I was doing fine on my own." An inner voice questioned, *Was I really?*

"It doesn't hurt to have them in your debt," my mother tsked, gesturing to my arm as she moved through the room toward the window. "Sorry about that. It was necessary for the ruse to be believable."

Frowning, I tried to clear my thoughts. It was beginning to feel like my skin was still on fire. But what she was saying… almost made sense. I shook my head. Maybe I was losing it too.

I followed her deeper into the room toward the

THE SECRET SHADOW

sole window, glancing over my shoulder anxiously. "This 'ruse' isn't going to last much longer. As soon as they figure out what—and who—you are, they'll throw us *both* in the dungeons."

She smiled as if I'd described a tea party. Reaching over, she tapped my chin lightly. "You're such a worrier," she teased. "You get that from your father." Tucking a stray piece of hair behind my ear, she added more seriously. "Your beauty and brains are all from me, though. Use them wisely, darling. And embrace that Gift. It'll do more for you than anyone here ever will."

Pulling the window open, she paused to add over her shoulder, "Unless you've changed your mind and would like to come with me to the human world after all? It's quite fun. *We* are the royals in their minds, and no one tells us what to do."

Mutely, I shook my head, frowning. "Even if I wanted to, we can't leave…?" I hadn't meant for it to come out as a question, but it did. The enchantment spell would stop her from using the window to escape—wouldn't it?

"I took care of that little problem right before you arrived to see the king and queen." She laughed. "Didn't you feel the spell lift?"

My mouth fell open. I *had* felt the bubble pop,

yet once again I hadn't recognized it. I'd attributed the reaction to my panic over what I'd been about to do. Looking back it was once again blatantly obvious.

My mother's short dress barely touched her thighs, exposing her long sandalled legs, as she lifted one foot up to the window and pulled herself onto the thin ledge. She hefted the bag over her shoulder and braced a hand against the frame, grinning at me. "Somewhere downstairs, there's a guard who'll wake up soon wondering why King Jubal commanded him to end the enchantment then knocked him out immediately after."

I met her smirk with a blank stare.

Even after the last few days with her, I still couldn't predict what she'd do. She moved faster than anyone I'd ever known.

Though we'd moved away from the hole in the floor, the crash of splintering wood and raised voices grew louder. They'd finally broken into the royal chambers.

She held out a hand. "Last chance, Jezebel."

My mouth opened and closed.

"I could teach you so many things," she whispered, hand still outstretched.

THE SECRET SHADOW

I bit my lip. Part of me wanted to go with her. To leave this place behind and start fresh...

It tempted me more than I'd expected it to.

Did I go back and face the royal family—now that they knew of my Gift and might imprison me for life, or equally awful, now that Shem might cast me out and never speak to me again? Or should I flee with my mother?

We'd spend the rest of our lives on the run, feared by everyone, unwanted.

Not to mention, she was a stranger to me.

It wasn't the life I'd dreamed of.

Staying here could be...

My muscles tensed, as if my body had already decided.

I had to stay.

Loud voices filled the room below. A door opened and closed. Probably the bathing room.

Queen Samaria's sobs reached us as she yelled at the guards, "Help the king!"

As soon as the king was deemed safe, they'd come for us.

For me.

They were probably on their way already.

Though I almost expected it to change my mind, it didn't. I couldn't imagine leaving.

"I can't," I whispered.

Despite everything, Shem was the one place where I'd truly belonged. He'd become my home. I couldn't leave him behind.

With a nod, my mother stepped down from the window and took my hand, giving it a squeeze. "I can't guarantee I'll come back in the next century," she said calmly. "But I'll try to visit once things have died down a bit."

She pulled the sharp spindle out of her pocket, turning my hand over.

I opened my fingers instinctively to accept it, but she didn't set it down.

When I glanced up, she was staring at me. "Do you remember how we met in the kitchen?"

I nodded warily. "When I tried to poison you?"

She surprised me by cracking a smile. "Exactly. What you should've used was a sleeping spell. It doesn't give a shifter time to fight it—"

Before I could react, she pricked my finger with the spindle.

Sleeping spell? My eyes widened.

A tiny spot of blood pooled on the tip.

I stared at it.

It was a tiny injury compared to the burns

covering my arm, yet I sensed it was about to get much worse.

"Don't worry," she murmured, pulling me into her arms for a one-sided hug. "It'll wear off within a few hours. Or days… I'm not entirely sure."

I couldn't fight back or even speak as my mother gently lowered me to the floor, as if she was simply putting me to bed the way she had when I was a little girl.

Disbelief stole my breath.

Or maybe it was whatever spell the spindle held. I could feel it entering my bloodstream at a rapid speed.

And then, I couldn't feel anything.

I never should've trusted her.

"I'm sorry this visit caused you so much trouble," my mother's voice whispered in my ear, but I found that I couldn't turn to look at her. Or lift my chin. Or move at all.

My breath came in great gulps now, eyes widening. Panic gripped me as even those small actions grew nearly impossible.

"We made it look good," were my mother's last words as she leaned over me, winking, before she stepped back toward the window.

Breathing hard, I felt a tear slip from one eye.

I never should've let my guard down.

I'd never forgive her.

The worst part was, I didn't know what hurt more, my future with Shem being ripped out of my grasp for the thousandth time, or my mother proving once again that she didn't care about me.

She never had.

With a glance over her shoulder, she shifted.

Voices grew louder behind me.

I couldn't turn to look, but I felt every shake of boots pounding on the floor.

My mother became a phoenix with red and gold feathers, perching on the window sill. In her beak, she gripped the bag. With a burst of wings flapping, she launched into the air.

From the floor, I couldn't see where she went.

Guards filled my vision, blocking the window. Maybe they chased her or threw a spear. I'd never know. My vision faded, growing black around the edges.

Someone grabbed me harshly by the wrist, restraining me, yelling to others.

The last thing I felt before I lost consciousness was a sharp tug as someone dragged me across the floor.

20

WHEN I CAME TO, Shem's face hovered above mine, dark brows pinched together. He hadn't been this close to me since we'd kissed. For a second I forgot everything that'd happened in between and just stared into his eyes. They reminded me of a cloudless summer sky. Warm. And open.

"You're okay," he breathed. "Can you speak?"

I tried, but I couldn't.

When I attempted to shake my head, I couldn't do that either. The looseness I'd felt a moment ago evaporated. My mind reacted violently, but any physical reaction was invisible.

"Blink if you're all right," Shem whispered.

Immediately, I blinked.

He let out a heavy breath, leaning back against the sofa, closing his eyes in relief. A second later, he stood, saying as he moved out of sight, "Let me get you something to drink."

I lay prone on a soft surface. Eyes shifting to one side, I found green cushions the same color as the green sofa where the king and queen had lounged earlier. Was I still in the royal chambers? How long had I been asleep?

My mother's wild outburst of shifting, thieving, and enchanting all came back to me in a rush.

Straining, I urged my body to sit up.

I could almost wiggle my toes.

Whatever the enchanted spindle had done, my mother had at least told the truth—it *was* wearing off, even if it was agonizingly slow.

My eyes flitted around the room, taking it in from this strange angle, searching for the king.

He'd been injured, badly.

If he didn't survive, I feared that I might not make it through the day either.

When I spied him on the opposite sofa, my

breath caught.

He was still. Pale.

I feared the worst until I noticed his chest moving in steady breaths.

An elderly Jinni hovered over him, tentatively pressing bony fingers around the king's shoulder, which looked swollen.

"Just do it," the king growled, eyes still closed, startling both me and the other Jinni. If I'd had control over my body, I would've flinched, but then relaxed.

The king was fine.

With a sharp yank, the healer popped King Jubal's arm back in the socket, causing the king to hiss in pain and then yell, "Enough. Leave me!"

Jumping to obey, the healer backed up, leaving my line of sight.

When Shem's face appeared over mine again, he held a glass of water and his gaze was pinned to my shoulder. "That looks painful."

I frowned. It didn't *feel* painful? Which was odd, because I remembered the burns and the way they'd set my body on fire.

Now there was only a slight tingling in my limbs.

Maybe that was the one upside of this enchanted

sleep—it'd removed *all* sensation from my body, including the pain, providing temporary relief.

"When the healer returns from fetching ice for your father, we'll have him see to her," Queen Samaria's voice came from somewhere above my head.

My eyes widened.

She was offering me their personal healer?

Maybe my mother's meddling had had better results than I'd expected. I wanted to shake my head and smile at the same time. I couldn't decide if I was thankful or annoyed. Or both.

Shem smiled slightly, and I realized it was in response to my own expression. The feeling was returning to my face.

He ignored the chaos surrounding his father—as healers and guards came and went, reporting on their findings in hushed voices—and just sat with me.

At some point, as sensation continued to return, I realized he was holding my hand. He gazed at our fingers, head bowed, deep in thought.

I squeezed his fingers weakly.

"Are you in pain?" he asked instantly, studying me.

Clearing my throat, I attempted to speak again.

"A little." I grimaced. My voice was ragged. Managing a wobbly smile, I forced myself to continue, "I'm so sorry. Truly."

"I know," he said, pulling my uninjured hand closer, taking care not to move abruptly.

"She's awake?" the king's gruff voice reached us.

This time, when I tried to turn my head to look, my neck slowly obeyed.

His sharp eyes dug into mine. "Where's the shifter?" he demanded.

"Gone, your highness," I croaked.

Another voice spoke up. "She watched the shifter fly off, your highness. Didn't even try to stop her."

I'd know that voice anywhere, especially after the interview that'd happened a few short hours ago.

Gabriel.

Another guard, whose voice I didn't recognize, chimed in, "To be fair, she'd clearly been immobilized by the spell. She was in no position to stop it."

Thank you, I wanted to say, but I held my tongue.

Shem leaned forward, but he wasn't looking at me. His gaze was pinned on his father. "We watched her—" his hesitation was so slight that anyone else besides his father, mother, and I would never guess he'd almost said "shift" before he caught himself—"step between us and the shifter."

Gesturing to my wounds, he added, "She *saved your life*."

I glanced down to see what he was pointing at. It made my stomach riot. I had to look away. The skin was exposed to the air by the burned remains of my dress, bubbling unnaturally, blistering red and even charred almost black in some places. I gagged softly. The pain increased tenfold once I'd seen it and now I was fully aware of the awful heat rippling across my skin.

"I know that," the king snapped, but behind him I caught multiple guards exchanging glances. They had *not* been aware. Their eyes drew to my injuries.

My mother had set this up for me.

Making me the victim had been a calculated move.

Despite the throbbing along my chest and arms growing with each passing second, I found myself grateful for the hurt.

Each time I thought I knew her plans, I was wrong. She thought a hundred steps ahead, while I only thought of what came next. Though she may never be an official mentor to me, I could still learn a thing or two from her.

If I wanted to benefit from this moment, I needed to begin thinking like her.

Removing all suspicion was the best place to start.

Everyone's eyes were on me.

As the pain intensified, I shivered. Moving as if to sit up, I fell back on the couch and let the throbbing bring tears to my eyes. It wasn't hard. In fact, it was growing increasingly hard to think past the pain.

"Stay still," Shem said, tightening his fingers around mine. "The healer is bringing ice that should help with your burns."

I nodded, clearing my throat, and let more tears fall as I said to the king, "I'm so sorry, your majesty." Turning my head back to Shem, I added, almost in a whisper, "I couldn't stop it."

Shem rubbed a thumb absently against my palm, and his face relaxed. It wasn't until I noticed the slightly vacant look in his eyes that I realized I'd accidentally used my new Gift on him. Again.

It wasn't on purpose. I cringed inwardly. *And it's the truth. So it doesn't count.*

King Jubal grumbled, but didn't question me

further.

"It's the fact that you tried to stop the shifter that impresses me," Shem said softly, brushing a hand over my cheek, careful not to graze the burns with his sleeve.

"You were all perfectly safe," Captain Uriel said in a soothing tone. "Your enchanted armor would've protected you, if this young lady had not gotten in the way."

When Shem turned to face him, his tone was like ice. "Those enchantments were useless. Look at my father." King Jubal, along with all the guards around us, glanced down at his ceremonial armor, where the ruby rested beside multiple scrapes and dents. "While you were all wasting time in the hallway, Jezebel fought the shape-shifter. She is the *only* reason we are all largely unharmed. Your disrespect is disgraceful."

The captain mumbled apologies to me, looking chastened. "I only meant the danger wasn't as awful as it may have felt."

When Shem merely glared at him, he cleared his throat and made his excuses to leave. As he bowed to the royals, he included me as well.

Gabriel stood posted by the door, within my

view from the sofa, and he looked down his nose at me, skeptical. He'd *just* completed my interview, which meant he knew all my Gifts—or thought he did. I could almost hear him wondering how someone with only a traveling Gift had stood up to a shape-shifter.

If I made it through this day without ending up in the dungeon, I'd make an effort to find him alone soon and *convince* him to leave the matter alone. Using my new Gift for that would be my one exception.

Fortunately, Gabriel remained silent for now. He wouldn't argue publicly with the prince, especially not after the way his captain had been reprimanded.

The remaining guards silently waited for a command.

Queen Samaria finally moved into my line of sight as she sank onto the sofa beside the king.

Both of them eyed me.

I tensed.

Please don't reveal my secrets, I tried to silently beg. The king's stern expression didn't change, and the queen was unreadable.

I'd never had a chance to tell them about the second Gift. But their awareness of my shape-shifting was enough. More than enough, if they decided I wasn't worth the risk.

Shem, on the other hand, knew *everything*.

He still sat close enough to hold my hand, pressing his palm into mine to offer silent strength.

As the king considered me, I forgot to breathe.

Finally, he turned to the guard. "The prince speaks the truth. This young Jinni was attacked first when the shifter struck. She fought back. It is to her credit that she stood between the awful creature and the royal family, and she is to be commended for her bravery."

He didn't mention my Gifts at all.

Queen Samaria, who'd been speaking with a servant, paused, then nodded.

She didn't say anything either.

When I turned to Shem, he gave me a subtle nod.

Fresh tears filled my eyes. When Shem brought my hand to his lips and kissed it, I couldn't stop them from streaming down my cheeks. He and the others called for the healer to hurry with the ice packs, which they gently placed over the burns, working to salvage enough of the skin for the healer's Gift to restore it.

Despite the agony, I was able to take a deep breath for the first time since the shifter's presence had been announced in the castle.

    I might still have a place here after all.

21

A FEW DAYS LATER, I paused at the grand entrance to the dining hall.

My wounds were fully mended, thanks to the healer's Gift.

Chandeliers sparkled, flashing bits of light across the high ceiling, which was painted with different scenes of Jinni history.

Every table was full. In the din of conversation, no one noticed me hovering outside in the hall. Members of the Guard were posted by the exits, and throughout the room, but no more than usual during an event like this.

In some ways, it was as if nothing had changed.

Yet despite the cheerful scene, everything was different.

All anyone wanted to talk about was the shifter, or how I'd fought against it, or my mother's dramatic exit. I didn't have to fight for a place at a table or in conversation anymore; people made room. They truly wanted to know me. And if, for some reason, someone didn't... A tiny smile touched my lips. If I truly wanted to, I could *make* them like me. Technically, I could force them do anything at all.

My new Gift tickled my mind at times like these, reminding me that I would never again have to suffer gossip or rude comments, if I didn't want to.

It was overwhelming.

And incredibly, wonderfully satisfying.

I'd never use it on Shem, of course, but he wouldn't care if I occasionally used it for our benefit, would he?

On the far side of the enormous room, the royal family all sat at their private table, surrounded by three separate tables for each of their councils. Each one was filled to capacity. Even from across the room, I spotted Milcah, Jerusha, Dorcas, Laban, and at least two dozen of Shem's other council members.

Every single council member I'd met in my time

at the castle was in attendance, as well as some I hadn't, who'd traveled back specifically for this occasion.

I brushed a hand down the floor length gown that the queen herself had commissioned for me. I was still in awe. The gold shimmered in the light, gleaming like a newly minted coin. Along one arm and leg, the fabric turned sheer with stunning golden spirals embroidered into the clear fabric, which ran all the way to my hip as well as across my collarbone like delicate gold lace.

Knowing the queen, she likely wanted the patterns in the lace to resemble the scars I'd had before my burns healed, as yet another reminder to everyone of what I'd done. As if anyone needed it.

When I stepped into the dining hall, a hush slowly took hold with each table I passed, until it crossed the entire vast space, causing all eyes to turn to me.

I kept my chin high, eyes forward.

Whispers tickled my ears.

The words weren't clear, but I didn't need to hear them to guess what they were saying: "How did *that* girl face a shifter?" and "What Gifts could she possibly have that allowed her to survive?"

Without meaning to, my gaze drifted slightly, to

the members of the Jinni Guard on duty along the back walls. They each stood stiff and composed. But rumors had probably begun to circulate in their barracks as well. Because *they* had a record somewhere, written and stored by Gabriel, listing exactly what Gifts I had.

Or at least, so they thought.

And while they'd never question the royal family outright, it had to be obvious to them that something didn't add up.

I reached the council members and stood before the dais that raised the royal family's table. In the corner of my eye, both Milcah and Jerusha seemed to eye my dress. I hoped they were jealous. I didn't dare look, keeping my gaze focused on the royals.

After my shoulder had finished healing, Shem had revealed that the king and queen chose to keep my secret at his request. He came by my room frequently, if I wasn't meeting with one or both of his parents.

I'd never had a chance to tell the king and queen about my second Gift, though. When I'd asked Shem to give me time to find the right words, he'd agreed without blinking an eye. I didn't *think* I'd used my Gift when I asked, but I wasn't entirely sure.

And none of them—not even Shem—knew that

the shifter was my mother.

It would only hurt him to know.

It seemed King Jubal liked the idea of having a secret shifter working for him behind the scenes. He had a gleam in his eye as he set his fork down to acknowledge me.

I stopped before the dais and bowed deeply.

As I sank low, I allowed myself to peek over at Shem's council table beneath my lashes. Milcah was flushed, and Jerusha's fists were clenched in her lap. I smiled to myself, lifting my gaze back to the king as I stood.

"Jezebel," his voice boomed, carrying throughout the whole room. "As this dinner is in your honor, we invite you to join us at our table." With a flourish, he motioned toward an empty seat beside his son.

Beside me, Milcah inhaled sharply through her teeth.

My cheeks dimpled with the effort of holding in a grin. Solemnly, I nodded my thanks.

Coming around the table, the chair beside Shem was so tall it looked like a throne. Before I could touch it, a member of the Guard stepped forward and pulled it out for me.

I sank onto the soft velvet cushion, barely

feeling it as I placed my hands on the white linen tablecloth.

Next to me, Shem gave me a wink, the way he used to, before I'd broken his trust.

A trust which seemed to truly be restored.

All around the room, everyone's eyes were on us. I hid a smile, tucking my napkin in my lap, enjoying the way Milcah fidgeted jealously with her own.

Clearing my throat, I accepted a plate of food from a servant and picked up my fork, but the king wasn't done with making proclamations. "Let's raise our glasses to Jezebel," he declared in a deep voice that carried over the still hushed room. "And rejoice that we are safe and the shifter is gone!"

A cheer erupted across the dining hall.

Though the Jinn were naturally reserved, we were too relieved to stand on ceremony tonight.

Drinks flowed, and courses came and went.

I barely had a chance to say two words to Shem, as different council members stopped by the table to speak with him and his parents.

I tried not to look at anyone in the Guard, but a prickling sensation on my neck made me feel like their eyes were on me.

According to Shem, they'd put new safeguards

in place to protect everyone in the castle from future attacks. Privately though, the king and queen had assured me that I wouldn't be affected by these changes. That I could come and go as I pleased without triggering any alerts.

I'd thanked them, glad that I didn't have to force them to trust me. Real trust was far more compelling. Although I wasn't above planting a false faith in me, if necessary. Sometimes I even contemplated telling them to forget what I'd revealed to them. I was still trying to find my footing in this new world where others *knew my Gifts.*

It was only Shem, the king, and the queen—and my mother. But what if one of them told someone else? With each passing day, I grew a little bolder. It couldn't hurt to use my Gift to enforce the secret, could it?

Yesterday, the healer had pronounced me officially restored, shaking Shem's hand as he'd left the royal chambers.

I'd tentatively caught Shem's hand before he followed and whispered, "Can I ask a favor?"

"Anything," he'd said instantly, smiling.

I'd glanced at the guards near the door and stood, drawing Shem toward the window where we wouldn't be overheard.

Tendrils of guilt had swirled around me as I'd used my new Gift on him intentionally for the first time. "It'd mean the world to me if you didn't discuss my… newest Gift with your parents. If they—"

I'd prepared a long explanation of how they didn't really need to know about my Gifts, besides shape-shifting, and how I didn't want anyone to accidentally overhear and discover, but he'd interrupted, "Of course. Your wish is my command."

I'd paused, studying his eyes for the vacant look that I was coming to recognize, but they'd twinkled slightly as he'd smiled, pressing his lips to my forehead. The warmth had made me flush. Those little attentions raised hopes that I was terrified to entertain, but too thrilled to fully ignore.

Now, beneath the banquet table—as the dessert course was served and Shem had a brief respite from conversation—he reached out to take my hand, curling his warm fingers over mine.

Leaning close, until his lips brushed my ear, he said softly, "I should've trusted you. You've always had my best interest at heart."

A twinge of guilt pinched me. He wouldn't trust me if he knew about my mother. Or about what'd happened to my friends when we first met. And I still wasn't sure whether or not I'd used my new Gift to keep him from telling his parents, or what he'd think if I used it to swear the king and queen to silence as well.

You've always had my best interest at heart.

I silently vowed to him that I would do exactly that going forward, including when I used my Gifts. Especially then. Nodding, I managed a small smile.

His chair squeaked against the floor as he shoved it back unexpectedly and stood.

"What're you doing?" I whispered, squeezing his fingers. I let go before anyone noticed that he'd held my hand.

"You'll see," he said with a grin and another wink.

Nearby tables grew quiet, but it wasn't until he used his silverware to clink against the glass that the stillness spread to the rest of the room.

He cleared his throat, drawing out the suspense.

What's going on?

Raising his voice so that the entire room could hear clearly, he addressed everyone, but kept his gaze on me. "Today we gather to honor someone who's grown to mean a great deal to me."

A buzzing lit in the back of my head, a tingling sensation that something big was coming. I didn't know what to expect. In all my time here, he'd never made an unrehearsed speech like this before.

"You've proven yourself to the royal family in a way that few ever will." His pale eyes were almost gray in the candlelight, flickering with an emotion I couldn't name. "More importantly, this latest crisis has revealed to me how much I've come to care for you."

Out of the corner of my eye, Jerusha's hand flew to her mouth. I snuck a glance at their table to find her sagging back in her chair. Milcah was as still as death.

My eyes flitted back to Shem.

I didn't know where this was going, but I sensed there was more.

For a long moment, he was quiet, staring into my eyes. I began to wonder if I should reply—then I caught the glisten of unshed tears. He was composing himself.

Reaching out, he took my hand gently.

I froze.

We'd never held hands publicly before. Was he making a declaration?

Squeezing my fingers lightly, he led me around the table to stand in front of it, before letting go.

He lowered himself to one knee.

All at once, I knew where this was going.

My hands flew to my cheeks, and I almost shook my head.

I hadn't dared to believe this could actually happen.

My heart beat unevenly.

"Jezebel," he said softly, not caring if anyone else could hear. "You really are a legend."

In the corner of my vision, his parents leaned closer.

Everyone was leaning in.

He rubbed a thumb across my hand. "Will you do me the honor of becoming my wife?"

My lips parted.

Is this real? I rapidly inventoried the last few days…

Was it was possible I'd somehow used my Gift to make this happen?

No.

I hadn't said a word that might lead him to this conclusion.

This is all him.

I blinked back happy tears as his face began to blur and nodded. "Yes. Yes, of course!"

He leapt to his feet, pulling me into his arms. The room broke out in cheering and applause. I laughed with him, allowing myself to feel truly happy for once.

This was real.

I hadn't forced this—not really.

A few secrets could hardly be considered an issue. Every Jinni had them.

Shem distracted me from my thoughts with a finger on my cheek, leaning in, until his lips were a breath away from mine.

"May I?" he whispered.

My whole body flushed.

He wanted to kiss me here, now, in front of everyone. There was no more pretending to be calm. I was smiling so wide my cheeks hurt as I closed the distance.

At first, he kissed me softly.

I threw my arms around his neck and leaned in.

He lifted me, deepening the kiss with a laugh, and as he lowered my feet back to the floor to the sound of thunderous applause, a new revelation hit me.

I'm marrying into the royal family...

I pulled back, staring into his handsome face, as the implications swept over me like shock waves.

The girl who didn't belong anywhere now had a permanent place at the heart of the kingdom.

I could hardly dare to think the words, but they

snuck in anyway, making me grin back at Shem.

Someday, I'll be queen.

THE END.

If you enjoyed this book, support the author by leaving a review!

The story continues in

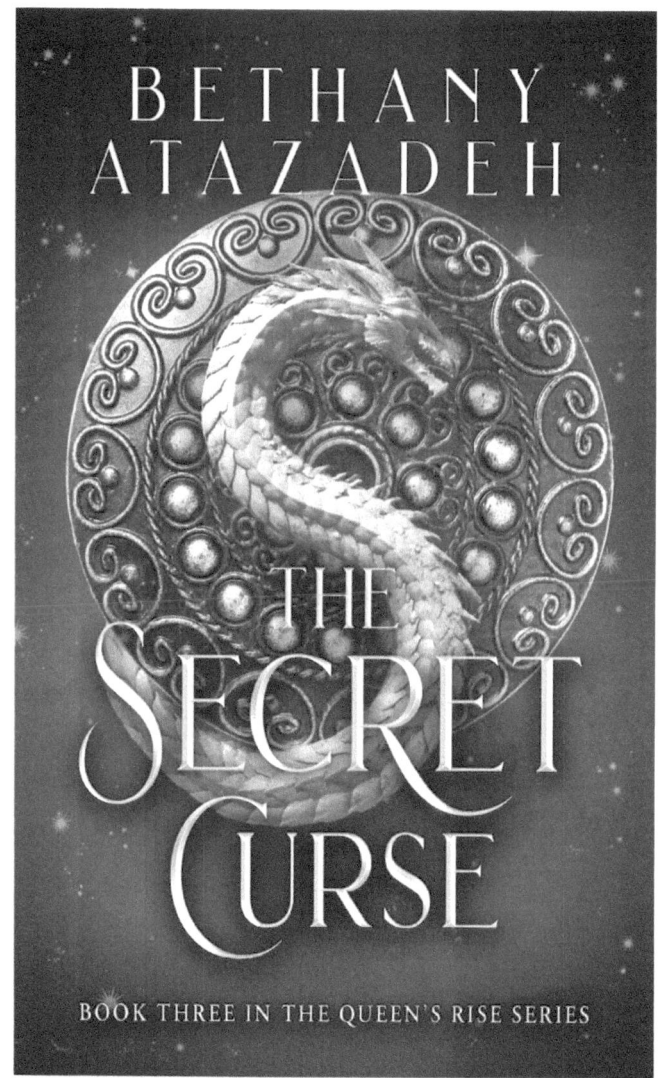

THE SECRET CURSE

Engaged to a prince, but not queen yet...

As Jezebel and the Jinni prince begin their engagement tour, the increasing attacks of the Khaanevaade hint at impending war. When these people attempt to kidnap the illusive prince of Jinn, Jezebel is captured—and taken instead.

Despite their fearsome dragon-like abilities, Jezebel believes she could easily save herself, if necessary. But first she hopes to learn the enemies' secrets. This way, she'll prove her worth to the royal family once she escapes.

Instead, she discovers the tribe's fierce hatred of all things Jinn, including her. The leader's son hates her most of all. Yet, as time passes, her handsome captor surprises her by being just as remarkable as the prince. Maybe even more so...

When the royal family makes a bargain that cuts her out of the picture completely, she begins to wonder if she truly wants a future with them at all, or if perhaps she wants to carve a new path of her own… with the enemy.

The Secret Curse **is the third and final book in** ***The Queen's Rise*** **series, inspired by your favorite villains in** ***Snow White, Sleeping Beauty, and Beauty and the Beast.*** **Over a century before Queen Jezebel crosses paths with Arie, Rena, and Nesrin, she's just an innocent Jinni girl… who was betrayed.**

READ THE SECRET CURSE NEXT…
books2read.com/thesecretcurse

SIGN UP FOR MY AUTHOR NEWSLETTER

Read the first half of The Stolen Kingdom for free, receive exclusive bonus content, a free short story, helpful tools for fellow writers, other behind the scenes updates, and more!

WWW.BETHANYATAZADEH.COM/CONTACT

GLOSSARY

Acropolis (Ah-CROP-oh-liss) – a wall surrounding the capital city Resh thick enough for thousands of Jinn to live in.

Council – each royal family members has a group of counselors that form a council, which they use for different political purposes.

Jezebel (JEZ-zuh-bell) – young Jinni shape-shifter

Jinn/Jinni (Gin/GIN-nee) – Jinn is the name of the country and the people of Jinn as a whole (i.e. *the Jinn, the land of Jinn*); Jinni is the singular, used to refer to an individual Jinni and also as a possessive (i.e. *a Jinni, a Jinni's Gift*)

Jinni Guard (GIN-nee Guard) – the dangerous and uniquely talented Jinn who guard the royal family

King Jubal (JOO-bull) – king of Jinn

Kathenoth – a journal used by paranoid Jinn with enemies meant for someone to read and remember them, if they are struck by a Shakach (forgetting spell) and vanish without a trace

Khaanevaade (Hah-nah-vah-DAY) –a people group even older than the Jinn, the supposed ancestors of dragons

Lacklore – a beast in Jinn with the head of an ox and the body of a bear

Prince Shem (Sheh-mm) – prince of Jinn

Queen Samaria (Saw-MARE-ree-uh) – queen of Jinn

Resh – capital city of Jinn

River Mem – the river that runs through the city of Resh

Severance – when a Jinni's Gift is severed from its owner

Shakach – a forbidden forgetting spell that means something between ignorance and withering, and erases a Jinni from existence completely, even in their own mind, as well as filling the hole they left behind until it's no longer noticeable

Traveling – a common Gift that allows Jinn to instantly cross an enormous distance in the span of a heartbeat

Three Unbreakable Laws of Jinn:

1) Never use a Gift to deceive
2) Never use a Gift to steal
3) Never use a Gift to harm another

ACKNOWLEDGMENTS

A huge thank you to:

My critique partners, Brittany Wang and Jessi Elliott!

My beta readers: Athena Marie, Katherine Schober, and Lia Anderson.

My cover designer, Mandi Lynn at Stone Ridge Books.

My patrons, for their financial support and faith in my work—I appreciate you more than you know, thank you for supporting my stories!

My family, who have supported me in so many ways, even little Zion who makes writing a whole new challenge! I wouldn't change it for a thing.

And you, my reader—thank you for taking a chance on this story. I hope you enjoyed Jezebel's and can't wait to hear what you think! Thank you in advance for every thoughtful review, sharing with friends, posting about it online, and making this book a success through your excitement. I couldn't do this without you!

Bethany Atazadeh is best known for her young adult fantasy novels, The Stolen Kingdom series, which won the Best YA Author 2020 Minnesota Author Project award. She is a mama to a cute little boy and a corgi pup, and is obsessed with stories and chocolate.

Using her degree in English with a creative writing emphasis, Bethany enjoys helping other writers through her YouTube aka "AuthorTube" writing channel and Patreon page.

If you want to know more about when Bethany's next book will come out, visit her website below where you can sign up to receive monthly emails with exciting news, updates, and book releases.

CONNECT WITH BETHANY:
Website: www.bethanyatazadeh.com
Instagram: @authorbethanyatazadeh
YouTube: www.youtube.com/bethanyatazadeh
Patreon: www.patreon.com/bethanyatazadeh

www.ingramcontent.com/pod-product-compliance
Lightning Source LLC
LaVergne TN
LVHW041748060526
838201LV00046B/950